Home
FOR THE
Holidays

Home
FOR THE
Holidays

CONNOR FALLS CHRISTMAS SERIES
NOVELLA

Robin Maderich

POTTER STREET BOOKS
ZIONSVILLE PA
2024

"At Christmas,
all roads lead
home."
— **Marjorie Holmes**

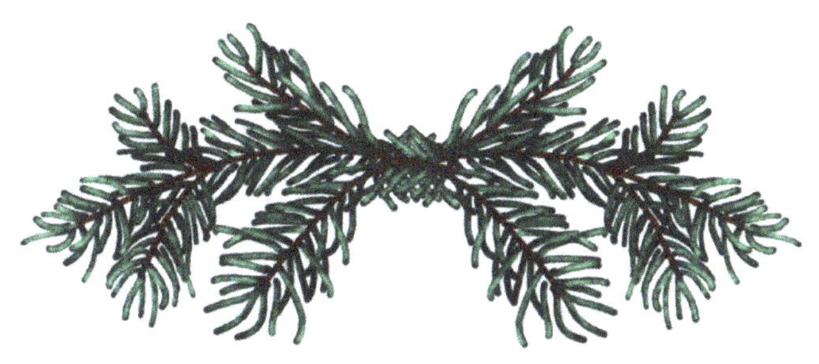

AUTHOR'S NOTE

I hope you enjoy this special, printed edition of *Home for the Holidays,* the third novella in the Connor Falls Christmas Collection, *When the Heart Brings You Home.* This one happens to be my favorite from the three. Something about the characters in it touch my heart in a special way.

Merry Christmas everyone. Curl up in a cozy place and read.

Yours,

Robin Maderich

Chapter One

Fallen leaves lay along the roadside in faded colors. At some point a light snowfall had coated the crisped brown edges with a sugar dusting, making me stupidly hungry, reminding me I'd skipped breakfast. I always told my clients, "Don't skip your morning meal, it sets the physical and mental tone for the rest of the day."

You think I'd have learned after all this time.

But no.

About a lot of things.

My phone trilled in the cup holder. I glanced down at the text from Mom and away. She could wait because a) I was driving, and b) I was almost there. Another five minutes and I'd be pulling into the driveway. A very long driveway, leading up to the expanded farmhouse she and Dad had purchased ten years earlier after selling the house nearby where we'd grown up. The house stood on about twenty acres a couple miles outside Connor Falls, bought with a dedicated plan to follow her midlife crisis dream. She'd not been wrong.

I spotted the sign for Hummingbird Farm. A new one, it looked like. Mom had been talking about a replacement and it seemed she'd taken care of getting one over the summer. I hadn't been to see Mom and Dad since springtime. I had a silent bet with myself this would be the first thing she mentioned. Not my haircut, not my new car, not the fact my brother only lived ten miles away and he probably hadn't been there since springtime either.

Turning into the driveway, I noticed the fields to either side pocked with cornstalk stubble. She and Dad didn't grow corn. They rented the fields by the road to

a local farmer. Those closer to the house were strategically planted each year with various sunflowers, zinnias, mums and other hardy flowers for cutting, as well as pumpkins and summer vegetables, the sorts Mom used in her business. What didn't get used she sold elsewhere or sometimes gave away. I caught sight of the ornamentals as I got closer to the house. Fall blooms in pots dotted the walkway together with white gourds that had somehow avoided damage from the recent freeze. At intervals between, small evergreen trees with burlap-wrapped root balls had been settled into metal buckets. Wreaths decorated the front windows on both floors as well as the front door, and a huge one had been affixed to the barn. Every year my dad climbed up on a ladder and hung the fresh greens. Every year I got pains in my chest thinking about him doing it. He wasn't getting any younger.

He'd get downright surly if he ever heard me say those words out loud, though, so I didn't. One day I'd have to. My brother darned well better make the ten-mile trek to join me for that conversation. Better still, he should come and hang the wreaths instead.

And maybe he did these days. We'd never talked about it.

Frowning, I pulled the car over into a "family"

spot. Parking spots were designated for us, for customers and for those utilizing the venue. Quaint little metal signs on black posts advertised these spaces clearly, pointing out who went where and how to get there. The signs for ours read Hardwick Family Only. Someone obviously couldn't read. I parked my car next to a dusty black Jeep with Delaware plates. Whoever they were, they hadn't come half as far as I had.

I eyed my short 'do in the visor mirror, spot-checked my teeth from force of habit since I hadn't eaten, then turned off the ignition before grabbing my purse and shoving my phone back into it. I'd leave my luggage in the trunk until later. The plan was for a longer than usual visit, up to the day after Christmas, so I'd brought two bags with me. No need to walk to the door encumbered since I anticipated hugs before being chastised for having stayed away since spring.

My boots crunched on the gravel, echoing off the beautiful red barn where events were held, from family reunions to weddings. The upcoming weekend's affair happened to be a wedding, holiday-themed and all. Mom had sent pictures of the planned décor, the bride's and bridesmaid's gowns. *You always wanted a winter wedding*, she'd written in her email. Yeah, when I was twelve and thought the whole thing would be

terribly romantic and beautiful.

Despite my cynicism, I still carried around the image in my head. The bridesmaids wore cranberry, the men ivory, long-tail tuxes. The flower girl I'd pictured with a delicate floral wreath on her head, skipping along the carpeted aisle in a leaf-green dress, tossing flowers here and there (what did I know? I'd been just a kid myself), while I dressed in a gown over which a forest green velvet cloak draped to the floor. The wide hood took a veil's place, my face hidden demurely within its folds. Poinsettias lined the aisle and evergreen draped each pew. I remembered there were lights, too, in my imaginings, warm white lights like on old-fashioned Christmas trees.

Egads. Really? I must have been watching too many Disney movies.

The front door opened before I'd mounted the porch steps, interrupting my thoughts. I expected my mother's face, but instead my gaze met the back of someone's head. A man, a bit tall, fumbled for the screen door handle behind him without turning. I heard my mother's voice in the shadowed hall beyond. I kept climbing, stopping at a safe distance from the swinging door and the man's anticipated exit.

"I'll see you in a few days, then," he said as he

stepped backward. I reached out a hand on the off chance he'd keep coming. He did. When my hand made contact with his back, he jumped a mile and spun around.

"Sorry," I said. "I didn't mean to startle you."

He rocked to one side and straightened, staring at me. I had the uncomfortable feeling he didn't know what to say. No problem would have worked, or that's okay. Or even, hi, I'm insert name here. Instead, his gaze shifted to my feet. He mumbled something unintelligible and darted past me and down the porch steps. Mouth open, I pivoted on my heel to watch him stride with an odd hurried gait across the gravel to the parked Jeep and climb inside. The engine revved. His face turned in my direction behind the closed window, hand lifting as he ducked his head in what I supposed might be a greeting or an apology, after which he backed the vehicle up and pulled away.

I turned to the door, to Mom standing there watching him, too.

"What on earth?" I said.

"Oh, don't mind him," she answered, stepping out.

"Who is that?"

Apparently too distracted for traditional hug-type hellos, she continued to look after his car as he made

his way to the driveway's end. "The new photographer I've been working with," she said. "Had you been here anytime in the past six months, you'd know."

And cha-ching. If I'd made a literal bet, I'd be rolling in the cash. Or not. Sure things didn't generally come with huge pay offs.

Mom reached out and grabbed me in a one-armed embrace. "Hello there, daughter. I like your hair. Come on inside. We're letting in the cold."

*   *   *

I trailed after her down the hall and into the humongous kitchen, also decorated for Christmas, including the equally humongous fireplace, big enough to roast a whole hog in if such were your fancy. Greens and holly hung from the mantel, giving off a wonderful scent.

I shirked off my coat, draped it on a chair, and headed for the coffee pot. I touched the Pyrex: still warm. Helping myself to a mug, I filled it halfway, dumped a hefty spoonful of sugar inside and headed for the fridge for some creamer. As I opened the door, I realized neither Mom nor I had yet said a word since I'd entered the house. If I lived there, this might have been considered halfway normal. But, as she'd reminded me, we hadn't physically been in each other's company in more than six months. Sticking my head inside the refrigerator, I checked the usual place for the creamer, then four more.

"So," I said, locating some half and half and sniffing the container to be certain the cream hadn't turned, "he travels an awful long way to take photos."

I heard a clank and pulled my head from the appliance. Mom had set a small metal pail on the kitchen table I hadn't even noticed she'd been carrying. Poking out from the top were the remains of what had once been fern leaves, dried on the plants to leafless but intricate design. They would make a pretty addition to the greens across the fireplace, I thought, and stopped myself. I'd never had a yearning to be crafty. I'd been trying to stifle it in my blood my whole life.

"What makes you think he's come a long way?"

"Delaware plates," I said, pouring enough half and half into my coffee to turn it a very light brown.

"Oh, I guess he hasn't taken care of it yet. He's been living in Pennsylvania for about seven or eight months now. In Connor Falls."

"Huh," I said, taking a sip from my mug and wrinkling my nose. "Someone who hasn't been born here actually moving to Connor Falls."

"What's wrong with that?" Mom asked, shooting

me a glance as she bent over the few ferns she'd spread out on the table. "It's a wonderful place."

"I know it is. I'm just wondering what would draw a person here. It's not a hotbed of industry. He couldn't have made the move on some vague hope he'd be guaranteed a living."

Mom drew a deep breath. I heard it across the room. "He was seeking peace and quiet," she said, her tone meant to shut me up. How long had she known me? That never worked.

"And what's his name?" I persisted. She looked at me again. "It's not like we were introduced," I reminded her.

"Arlo. His name is Arlo."

I slugged down more coffee. What I really needed was food. "Like Guthrie?" My mind went to a finch I'd once had, when I was ten.

"Like Guthrie," she said. Shoving the ferns back into the bucket, she exited with it, stage left. I followed.

"Where are you going with that? Do you need some help?" I called after her. When she didn't answer, I pursued a different path. "Why is Arlo looking for peace and quiet?"

She stopped dead, pivoting on her heel to face me. "Because he needs it. If you want to know more, you'll

have to ask him.”

“I don’t know him.”

“You would,” she said, “if you came home more than twice a year.”

Ouch. Twice in fifteen minutes. “We talk all the time, you and I. That counts.”

Her shoulders dropped. With her free hand she pushed hair loosened from her ponytail away from her face. The sunshine through the rear door highlighted the silver in the russet brown, the laugh lines at her eyes, the slight crease in her brow. Really, she hadn’t changed much at all since I was a kid. People said I looked like her. I should be so lucky.

“You’re right, Suze,” she said. “I’m sorry. I’m just a bit stressed about the wedding this weekend.” She shrugged, lifting her shoulder toward her ear. I stepped forward, grabbing the fern bucket.

“Well, I’m here now. What are children for, if not to be at their parents’ beck and call?” I smiled at her and kissed her cheek, breathing in the fragrance of her shampoo. “What are you washing your hair with these days? Smells delicious.” I pulled away and moved with her toward the enclosed back porch.

"Do you like it?" she asked, tossing her ponytail so the scent wafted my way once more. "I make it myself."

"Of course you do, Mom," I said.

Generally speaking, my mom possessed the ability to do just about anything she set her mind to. The words "no, you can't" had been eradicated from her mindset while still in the womb. If she hadn't already learned a skill through osmosis, she set out to acquire it.

I found myself painfully reminded of this fact when I stepped out onto the porch and spied row after row of beautifully arranged centerpieces on wooden trestle tables, each one fabricated with items from the garden, the woods, the fields, and local markets. I wouldn't even know where to begin. But once Mom had decided to start this business of hers, and convinced Dad it would be worth his while, too, she'd set about gathering the knowledge to perform every aspect herself. Not that she did it all. That would be too much. For one, it hadn't been long before she'd turned over feeding the attendees at barn events to caterers. However, before doing so, she'd gone from the simple meals she'd raised us on to complex gastronomy.

She often tired me out just watching her. Maybe I kept my visits to a minimum for good reason. Not true, of course. The winds of change were drifting into my sails.

"You creative types make me sick," I said.

Mom snorted.

"Seriously, though, those are gorgeous."

Hands on hips, she eyeballed her creations. "I've been tossing around the idea of teaching a course on how to make table centerpieces like these in January, when things slow down."

"Okay, now you're just showing off." I plopped the bucket on the nearest table.

With a laugh, she scooped the ferns out and carried them over to a table with a much-painted expanse of cardboard covering its length. She glanced back. "You look nice. You might want to change if you're going to help me."

Her smock hung nearby. Since she happened to be wearing a ratty sweatshirt, I took the smock down and slipped the stained, paint-spattered garment over my sixty-dollar sweater. "I'm good," I said.

Mom handed me a can. I turned it over, reading

the label. "Metallic-red spray paint? Don't you usually keep these things natural?"

"The bride wants some glitz."

Alerted by her change in timbre to a lower register, I shook the can and popped off the cap without further comment. Mom pushed some latex gloves at me. I tugged them on. Side by side, we merrily transformed elements that had been a deep, lovely brown into a color resembling a soda can, hanging them to dry by clothespins on an overhead line as we went along.

"So tell me more about this friend of yours," I said while we worked.

"The bride? I hardly know her." Again, that tone.

"I mean Arlo. I can tell you're fond of him. How did you end up deciding to use him for events? How did he even find you?"

She clipped another gleaming fern to the twine before answering. "I'd been advertising, after Debbie gave notice. He had references."

She seemed to be holding something back. "Is he like my age?" I asked, trying to draw her out. "Does Dad know you have a thing for a younger man?"

"Susan!"

"Kidding, Mom. I'm only making conversation."

"You're only being nosy," she said.

"Could be," I agreed, "but after the way he practically ran from me outside, I have a right to be curious."

"No," she said, "you don't. Like I said, you have questions ask him next time he's here, which will probably be the day before the wedding. He deserves that courtesy. I won't talk about him behind his back."

I blew a long breath out over my lips and returned to shaking and spraying and hanging in silence, but I couldn't hold out for long. "Tell me about the bride then. Her, you don't like. I'm sure you'll spill about her."

Releasing a resigned chuckle, she did. In detail and warming to the subject to the point she set down her paint can and forgot about the ferns. The bride, in her mid-thirties and therefore ought to be knowing better according to Mom, had been understandably fussy in the beginning, but over the past several weeks had called with countless changes, to everything.

"Are you charging her for these alterations?" I

asked.

"I wasn't, but I'm going to have to. It's in the contract that I can. The wedding and reception are this weekend and these changes may end up being costly, if they can even be accomplished." She pushed her hair away with her forearm and reached for her paint can, looking with surprise at the now empty table and the bright red desiccated ferns drying overhead. I snapped off my gloves.

"All done," I said. "I'm assuming this, too, was last minute."

"Uh-huh."

I shook my head. "I don't know how you do it."

"I don't know how you do what you do," she said. "I love my work, all of it, even with the issues."

"Are you thinking I don't?" I asked, but gently. I only wanted to make sure I understood her meaning.

"That's not what I'm saying, no." She took off her own gloves, laid them down on the cardboard to dry and reuse, and then switched a small oscillating fan on low to move the air around. "But do you? I'm just curious. Do you? We've never really discussed your feelings for your job in detail. I only know it took you…away."

My lip quivered, like I was two. I turned my attention to the gloves I'd cast aside, trying to straighten them out for re-use as Mom had done. She focused her attention on returning the spray paint to the shelf beneath the table, giving me a moment.

"I like what I do," I said finally, abandoning the fidgety latex. "I don't love it. I never imagined I'd love it, but I'm really good at it. Like you. I just don't have the added bonus of love."

In more ways, I realized, than one. I wondered where Dad was. I asked.

"He had to run to the rental store for table linens. Apparently white no longer works."

"Ugh," I said. We both laughed.

It was good to be home.

Chapter Two

My older brother had been residing in England for work the past three years. Mom never complained about his infrequent visits. Having an ocean between them made all the difference, I suppose. However, in the morning, my younger brother Simon drove over from his whopping ten miles away. We had the same initials, Shepherd, Simon and I, including middle names. We were the SHH. Mom and Dad thought giving us those initials hilarious, like a perpetual shushing.

I met Simon outside in the driveway as I headed into the barn carrying replacement linens from the back seat of Dad's car. Simon and I kissed and hugged awkwardly around the tablecloths before dividing the load in half. He followed me into the cavernous space carrying his portion which, I have to say, I made sure was larger than my own.

He'd been a tall, gangly kid and had become a tall, gangly adult with two tall, gangly kids, ages seven and nine. They took after Dad, my Gran said last time we were all together, like lick on spit. I'd never heard the saying before, but I do remember I almost split my jeans laughing. I stood beside him now, looking up at his face, the rafters behind his head whitewashed and lined with tiny, clear LED lights.

"It's pretty amazing what they've got going here, isn't it?" I said.

His mouth twisted: Dad's mouth. "You're just noticing this now?" he drawled.

"Let's just say I'm really recognizing it now."

His ruddy eyebrows lifted and he turned on his heel, looking up at the ceiling, then the tables and

chairs folded and piled against the wall. "Maybe we should set these out?"

"Not right this second," I said. "There's fresh coffee inside and I ran out earlier and picked up some baked goods from Gina's."

"What time was that?"

"About six."

"You were actually up at six?"

"Ha-ha. That's when the bakery opens. I like warm donuts. This is the only time I allow myself to eat them, when I'm home."

"You'll need a nap soon."

"Nope," I said.

"How much coffee have you had already?"

"Enough."

We looped our arms together and headed back to the house doing a fair imitation of Dorothy Gale and her lanky, straw-stuffed companion skipping along the yellow brick road. When we were halfway across the large graveled lot, I glimpsed Arlo's black Jeep parked between my car and Simon's. He still sat inside, silhouetted against the cold morning sun. I stopped, jerking my brother to a halt.

"Arlo," I said.

"You've met him, then?"

"Not yet." Releasing Simon's arm, I marched over to Arlo's vehicle and paused beside it, tapping on the driver's door window. His reaction was immediate and alarming.

"Oh, no, oh, no," I said, knees bending to bring my head closer to the glass. "I'm sorry! I didn't mean to startle you again!" I grabbed for the door handle. He beat me to it, pushing the door open. I jumped back before the door struck me, although it probably wouldn't have. I only imagined it might, based on his abrupt movements.

"You shouldn't do that," he stated.

"Shouldn't do which? Tap on the glass or try to open the door?" I felt suddenly off-kilter and defensive. I hadn't done anything wrong. I knew I hadn't, yet it seemed as though I'd been accused.

"Tap on the glass," he said. "You did startle me."

I sucked in a breath, took another step backward. He exited the Jeep and stood, tall enough I had to tip my chin way up to look him in the face. A puffing breeze tossed his very dark hair across his eyes. He shoved the strands from his forehead, his gaze on the ground.

"Is Mrs. Hardwick in? Mary?"

"My mother, you mean?"

"Yes," he said, much as if he didn't recognize the slight sarcasm I meant to convey. He met my gaze with a brief glance and quickly looked away to the front door. "I know you're her daughter. You look just like her."

"I, uh, well yes," I stammered. "She's inside."

He swung the Jeep door shut and strode past me, taking the porch steps crookedly and two at a time, like a man in a hurry. Opening the screen door, he knocked with his fist on the wooden one. Several seconds later Mom opened it, ushering him inside.

"What is up with that guy?" I asked the air in general. My brother answered.

"It's a long story and not mine to tell. You should probably ask him."

I should ask him. *I* should ask him. I didn't know him well enough to ask him any personal questions and our interactions seemed to indicate to me I never would. Simon and I trailed after Arlo into the house, where we both headed for the kitchen, the coffee and the fragrant donuts calling my name. Mom's voice and Arlo's drifted in from the enclosed back porch. I couldn't quite hear what they were saying with Simon going on about the kids and the upcoming Christmas play, I understood my opportunity for eavesdropping

was nil. Not that I engaged in that sort of thing. Not usually anyway.

I jerked my head toward the hallway leading to the back door. "Maybe they'd like something? Should I go offer?"

"Suze," Simon said in response, "you're incorrigible."

"Incorrigible? Is that a word we're using nowadays?"

"If the shoe fits," he said.

"Idioms, too. You're getting old." Ignoring his smug expression, I arranged a few pastries on a plate, gathered up some napkins and made my way to the porch. I peeked through the door panes before entering. Arlo and Mom stood side by side, attention drawn to something Arlo appeared to have placed among the centerpieces on the table. Dipping my head to the side, I glimpsed a few photographs. I elbowed my way in through the partially open door and held out the platter.

Mom glanced up. "Sweetie, how thoughtful. Thank you. Arlo, would you care for a pastry?"

He did care for one, although he didn't say so. He waited until I neared and offered him a napkin, which he took, as well as an éclair.

"Thank you," he said, not quite looking at me.

"I don't think you've been introduced to my daughter," Mom said. "Arlo, this is Susan. Suze, this is Arlo Woods."

"In the driveway," he said. "We sort of met in the driveway when she knocked on the glass." He turned to me and held out his éclair-free hand. I took it, slipping my fingers into his grasp. He shook my hand, a nice warm shake, the kind I liked. I hated it when men barely gripped your hand as though they feared they might break you.

"I'm sorry," I started, but he interrupted me, too.

"Don't be. Don't be sorry. It's not your fault I'm like this."

When his gaze met mine, my breath hitched. I dropped his hand and almost dropped the plate. He caught it as it slipped, settling the dish gently back onto my palm, all pastries still intact. I hooked my thumb over the edge.

"It's nice to meet you, Arlo," I said.

"Likewise, Susan," he answered with an odd formality belied by his twisting lips.

Confounded and actually blushing, I hastened back to the kitchen.

*　*　*

In my other life, my real life, I coached and

supported people with eating disorders, and here I stood, stuffing in a third donut. Thank goodness my clients couldn't see me. Even so, I felt as though I betrayed their trust by my actions somehow. To make matters worse, Mom caught me at it. She didn't say anything, though, didn't even give me one of her looks. She probably had no idea I was on my third. Either that or she understood chastising someone for their eating habits never did anyone any good.

"Whatcha got there?" I asked, jutting my chin at the photos in her hand. Arlo had left. I had seen him walking by, heard the front door open and close. I'd almost gone after him, to try once more to engage him in something resembling conversation.

"Arlo brought these over. The bride—"

"Does she not have a name, or did her parents christen her 'bride' in anticipation of her future calling?"

Mom's lips curved in a tired attempt at a smile. "She has a name. I just don't want to use it right now."

I wiped a crumb from the corner of my mouth and nodded in understanding.

"Anyway," Mom went on, "she wanted to see more sample poses. More than the other hundred she's already seen. I have a thumb drive with digital copies

on it. I'll email them over to her in a little bit. Any coffee left?"

I took her washed cup from the drain board and poured her some, no sugar, creamer a miniscule splash. "When did the bride advise you of this new demand?"

Mom took the mug from my hand and held it to her nose, breathing deeply. "Last night," she said. "Texted me around ten-thirty."

"Ten-thirty?" I echoed. "Are you kidding? Whose spoiled child is she? Do I know her?"

Mom shook her head, possibly disinclined to tell me in fear she'd further prejudice me against the poor darling.

"If she calls again, let me handle her," I said.

"That would be something to witness, certainly, but the day is nearly here. There's not much more she can alter at this point."

"Okay," I said, "but you know, if you need me, I've got your back."

She laughed out loud, reaching past me for a sweet concoction. "You better wrap these and put them away for Simon to take home to the kids," she mumbled around a mouthful. "Where's he gotten to, by the way?"

"The barn, maybe? He was eyeballing those tables

when we were out there."

With a sticky noise halfway between a moan and a garbled cry, Mom led the charge from the kitchen, I figured to stop Simon in his tracks. I trotted to keep up with her. Simon might look like Dad, but unlike our father he loved to take control. Even I knew the tables did not come down for dressing until the morning of the event. Other things needed to be cleaned, moved, shoved, placed and perfected before crowding the floor with seating.

I skidded to a halt behind Mom in the open barn doorway. Inside, Simon and Arlo conversed with interspersed grunts. Table legs thumped the floor. We peered through into the interior. Nearly all the tables had been set in place. I fully expected Mom to lose it, what with the bride's harassment already fraying her nerves. Instead, her lips curved, slowly, her expression holding a mixture of sad and happy.

"It doesn't matter," she whispered.

I had a suspicion she didn't mean for me to hear her words.

My brother spied her in the shadows. Arlo turned at his expression, following his gaze. Both saw Mom, but not me yet. I stayed in the shadows when she went forward. Arlo looked at her briefly before he slid his

eyes away. So it wasn't only me. A little slower than with me, but he did it with her, too. Habit, maybe? It seemed an odd type of habit to develop.

Yet he turned back a few seconds later, the smile he now offered bright and astoundingly engaging. "I hope you don't mind I gave Simon a hand. He looked like he could use one."

Simon laughed, clapped him on the shoulder. I saw him flinch, recover himself, smile again, a bit more cautiously this time. Mom took his hand in both of hers and held on a moment.

"Thanks," she said.

He shrugged. "Anything else I can do let me know."

"I'll keep you to that."

"Please," he said, quite solemnly, "do."

Mom dropped her hands and stepped aside as he started to circle around her. He gave both Simon and Mom a nod before heading toward the door where I still stood being nosy, discovering too late I couldn't duck into hiding. I'd already learned sudden movements and abrupt noises around Arlo weren't good, so I stood my ground and waited.

He paused next to me, head up, squinting toward the chilly sunshine outside. His dark hair curled at the

ends, right over his coat collar. His left hand he'd stuck in his pocket. The other he held out a little from his side, palm parallel to the ground.

"How long are you staying?" he asked.

"Until the day after Christmas," I whispered. Why was I whispering?

"Good," he said and left, walking over to his Jeep, climbing inside. He drove away without another glance in my direction. I let out a breath, not realizing until that moment I'd been holding it. Behind me, Mom and Simon had entered into a discussion about leaving the chairs go until she'd had a chance to do some other things in there. He agreed, said he'd be back on Saturday morning to get them set up. She thanked him then for helping Dad with the wreaths again this year. Again. I turned around and caught my brother's eye, smiling at him from across the room.

"So what's next on the agenda?" I asked, striding over to them, trying to dismiss the fact Arlo thought it a good thing I'd be sticking around for a while. Perhaps he didn't. Perhaps the odd exchange was only his way of making a stab at conversation. I couldn't help but wonder if he'd always been this way.

Simon rolled his eyes. "Oh, you're going to be sorry you asked her that. Mom probably has a list a

mile long."

Mom reached into her coat pocket. She pulled out a list, a literal list, creased and folded and a little grimy. Her fingerprints marred one edge, made bright by the red paint we'd used yesterday. If she murdered anyone with that list she'd be sunk. Whipping a pencil from her other pocket, she snapped the paper semi-flat and used the point to tap each item.

I met Simon's no-longer-rolling eyes. "This is your fault."

"I know," he said, "but you encouraged her."

Mom ignored us. She reached the list's end, flipped the paper over and back again. "I think we're good." She looked from my face to my brother's. "For now."

"Hallelujah," said Simon. "I've got to get home anyway. Kids have early dismissal."

Simon worked from the house most days now. Lucy commuted an hour each way to her job. They'd been lucky enough to find a way for Simon to be there when their sons returned from school. I admired their relationship, Simon's and Lucy's, the practical way they worked together toward solutions to benefit their family. It wasn't always easy, and it wasn't always possible. Mom and Dad were like that, too. Shepherd

and I, well, not so much. Not that we had families. Shepherd had a wife, though, Malory, a woman he'd met and recently married in London. No one had been able to travel to England for the event on such short notice. I'd been hoping they'd make it back here for Christmas. No such luck. Not this year. I knew Mom was disappointed. So was I.

"I'm going to head into town for a bit then," I said. "I've got some Christmas shopping to finish." They both gaped at me as if I'd sprouted a gross and unnatural rash. "What? I'm not like you guys. I'm ill-prepared, remember? The last minute thing is my fun."

They waved me off in dismissal. I scurried to the house to retrieve my purse and keys and to check if I remembered to comb my hair this morning. I didn't always.

By the time I came out, Simon's car had disappeared and Mom stood on the walkway frowning at a text on her phone. She glanced up at me.

"I'm not even answering this one."

"Good for you," I said. "Do you need anything while I'm out?"

"Coffee creamer. I know that half and half isn't your thing."

"I don't need it," I argued. She really didn't have

to cater to me. She had enough going on.

"Your brother likes it, too."

"Well alright, then, that's settled. Creamer it is." I patted her arm and continued down the walkway, stopping after another few feet when she called me. I pivoted on my heel, eyebrows arched.

"I love you, Suze."

I melted inside. "I love you, too, Mom."

"Try to be home for dinner. I'm making your Dad's favorite."

"Will do," I said, vowing to be back early enough to lend a hand. With a little wave, Mom turned and made her way up the steps and into the house. She didn't look back or she'd have found me still standing there. I couldn't imagine what she would have seen on my face. Biting my lip, I headed to my car and town.

*   *   *

I made my first stop the bookstore. I had little time if I wanted to make it back to the house to help with dinner preparations. Like Mom, I also possessed a list. One I'd made yesterday morning on a torn envelope before getting in the car.

To accompany what I'd already bought and wrapped, I wanted a book each for Sammy and Stuart. My brother had continued the Hardwick tradition naming his sons. I asked myself why, constantly. What I hadn't asked was what the boys were into these days, reading-wise. I ended up taking longer than anticipated trying to come to a decision regarding proper material. Despite my eleventh-hour tendencies, I didn't like to grab without thought. I enjoyed buying Christmas gifts. I enjoyed making them special. After seeking assistance from some guy named Todd stacking books, a most helpful individual, I exited the store with my purchases and moved on, checking my list again.

I had Mom, I had Dad. I had also previously mailed two lovely art journals to Shepherd and Malory at their new address. I still needed Simon and Lucy and one more for Mom, a little gift, something special. Lucy loved candles, raved about a store that had opened in town fairly recently. I went there next, walking straight up to the woman behind the counter.

"Do you know Lucy Hardwick?" I asked.

The woman looked taken aback. Recovering, she smiled. "She's a customer."

"Good. I'm her sister-in-law, and I want to get her a candle, but I don't want to get her one she's already bought. I know she shops here. She talks about it all the time."

"That's wonderful," she said. "Tell her I said thank

you."

"I will. You're the owner?"

"That's me. The Sophie in Sophie's Chandlery." She grinned. "And I think I have the exact candle for you. It's not a Christmas scent. Were you looking for a holiday fragrance?"

I told her I was not. She guided me over to a display on a side wall, lifted a candle from its place, popped off the glass lid and held the container out. I took it, leaning in close, but not too close, and breathed. Instantly I found myself transported to someplace warm, tropical and embracing.

"Perfect," I said. Lucy loved southern beaches.

"There's a matching soap."

"I'll take that, too."

"Gift wrapped?"

"Sure. Thank you." While she packaged and wrapped the soap and candle, I wandered around the store looking at the various hand-painted furnishings. I only knew they were painted by hand because the little card on each told me so. The pieces were impeccably executed. "These are lovely," I said. "Do you—"

I stopped, backtracked, snatched up a small wooden box from the tabletop where it had been nearly lost. Exquisite flowers had been painted on a green-

stained background, a ruby-throated hummingbird fluttering delicately over one. Not for nothing had my mother named the place she and Dad bought Hummingbird Farm. Every year she cleaned and placed dozens of hummingbird feeders in her gardens and they came in droves, so many that sometimes the air filled with a sound nearly beyond hearing from their tiny wings. When she managed a good long break in her day, Mom would watch them for hours. She'd captured them in photos small and large, framed and hung around the house.

"I'll take this, too," I said. This was more perfect than Lucy's candle. More perfect than anything. Mom would love it.

Satisfied and with only one more gift to pick up, I headed back to Main Street. In the world of gift-giving, Simon remained a conundrum. I really had no idea what to get him. Lucy hadn't been able to help when I asked. She was finding herself in the same position. We all did, every year. So, I peered for inspiration into every window I passed, moving little by little toward Hannah's. The department store had been founded long before my parents were born, surviving through periods of economic upheaval and still strong. Its endurance remained a point of pride among the older Connor

Falls' residents, as if they had singlehandedly managed to keep it going. Still, I didn't want to shop in there. Not today. I didn't want to buy Simon a nice shirt or a tie—especially since he rarely wore either these days—but something more personal.

I slowed to a halt at the corner, my thoughts clicking away on ideas. Pulling out my phone, I checked the time. My gaze snapped to the sidewalk in front of Hannah's decorated windows. Several people gasped at the same time I noted Arlo bent double like he'd been pole-axed at the waist, his right arm extended and hand spread flat on the sidewalk. Slowly he righted himself. He stood a moment, settling himself into place, murmuring to those who offered to help him as he waved them away. His eye briefly caught mine.

I couldn't have felt worse. I recognized his fervent wish to be anyplace else but there. Hoisting my packages, I darted across the street and up to him.

"Are you okay?"

"Yeah," he said, "thanks." He turned on his heel, checked with his arms out slightly from his side, and a moment later started walking in the opposite direction he'd appeared to have been headed. I fell in beside him, not caring whether he wanted me there or not.

"Where are you going?" I asked.

"Home."

"I'll walk with you, if that's okay."

"You're already walking with me," he said. "You don't have to. I'm fine now. Even if I wasn't…" He let the sentence hang, walking with his head up and his brown eyes holding steady on a distant point.

"What happened?"

"Just now?"

"Yes," I said, thinking *as opposed to when?*

"I gave up my cane a few months ago. This hardly happens anymore. I'm good at catching myself."

Not an answer, Arlo. Not a direct one, anyway. "Is that why you walk with your hand out a bit? Because your hand is used to a cane?"

"Everything takes a lot of concentration some days," he said. "Even now. Even talking."

I took the hint and shut up, moving with him in silence. After a few minutes his stride steadied, his pace increasing. Not outstripping mine, by any means. He didn't seem inclined to race away. His gaze still held tight to that isolated point somewhere ahead.

"The most insidious injuries are those others can't see."

I shot a sideways glance at him, unsure if he wanted me to question that, or if he'd only uttered those

words as a general complaint to the universe. Suddenly, though, I got it. I understood.

"How did it happen?" I asked.

"Car accident. Nothing broken, except my brain."

"I'm sorry," I said quietly.

"Don't be. I'm getting better."

I nodded, not speaking, mulling over how sorry I felt, not for him, but about what had happened to bring him to this…whatever it was exactly. We'd walked another block on the quiet side street when he halted on the sidewalk, resting his hand on a white wooden fence. I stopped beside him.

"This is it," he said. "My house. You've walked me home."

I looked up, startled. I hadn't been spending any time picturing Arlo's home, but if I had been, it wouldn't have been this. I studied the house's façade, a quaint bungalow similar to many others inhabiting the back streets as you got away from the lovely and simple Folk Victorians on either side of Main. White siding, black shutters, a paver walkway curved to the front door surrounded by carefully tended grass and a few strategically placed evergreen bushes. In summertime, flowers probably filled the pots on the little porch. Right now, they stood empty, one to each

side.

"Well, okay then," I said awkwardly. Should I make sure he got inside okay? I doubted it. Whatever had nearly taken him down fifteen minutes earlier seemed to have relaxed its grip. I had no idea if he'd accept the offer, or if it might outright offend him. Pretending to shuffle my bags, I eyed him from beneath my lashes. I found him staring at the sidewalk near my boot tips. He glanced up, met my gaze and moved on.

Time enough, though, to recognize what I'd witnessed earlier when Mom introduced us. Arlo Wood possessed profound determination in the most beautiful eyes I'd ever seen.

Chapter Three

Some people unnerved you with their constant staring. What was the opposite of that? Arlo. He didn't stare at all. His gaze constantly went elsewhere, like to my feet, or past my head, or sometimes, I'd noticed, his eyes closed when he spoke, as if in concentration. Probably was in concentration, given the brief reference to a brain

injury. I had no idea what he saw behind his lids. I wanted to. I wanted to understand his thoughts, his life. With further consideration—what I mustered up between climbing into my car and reaching the halfway point to Mom and Dad's—I decided my interest made sense. Arlo held an important place in my mother's life. My family knew him well. The color and shape and deep conviction in his eyes were and should be secondary to such plausible analysis.

Yes, this was what I told myself. By the time I pulled into a family parking spot, however, I'd begun to question my ability to reason.

I found Mom sitting on the front porch steps, her face to the sun. The day's temperature was far from warm, but the sun did feel good. I joined her.

"What's up?" I asked, setting my bags onto the step beside me. "Bride-alert?"

"Nope," Mom said without lowering her head, her lids shuttering her eyes. "Nothing since the earlier text. Which, I'll have you know, I did not answer."

"So, what are you doing, getting a dose of vitamin D?"

She grunted in a not-quite-committed way.

I fitted my hands together around my knee, studying the empty fields through narrowed lids. "I ran into Arlo while I was out."

Another grunt. Maybe she didn't want to know. Maybe she only wanted to sit in the sun in silence, undisturbed. I started to get up.

"Go on," she said.

I sat back down. "He told me about the accident. Well, that he'd had one. No details, but that's okay. I don't really need them."

"Good."

"He's getting better though, right?" I persisted, despite her closed eyes and limited responses. "That's the impression I got anyway."

"Yes."

Okay. I got up again.

"It's been a long road," she added, rising to an abrupt upright position beside me. She brushed the loosened strands from her ponytail away from her face. "He's a good man, Arlo is. Come on, let's get dinner started. Your dad will be home soon."

I gathered my packages, hopped up the last step and opened the door for her. She paused before going in, eyeing my bags.

"Did you get all your shopping done?"

"All except Simon," I said.

"Good luck."

"Did he tell you what he might like?"

She gave me an 'are you kidding' look and marched inside.

Dinner preparation required music blaring and lots of singing. It had always been this way. I still turned on my old cd player when I made my own dinner. It seemed too quiet otherwise. I wondered as Mom and I danced around with vegetables in our hands how Arlo would fare in this environment. He seemed ill-equipped in his present condition for loud noise. To me, his condition also seemed to isolate him. I might have been wrong. Even so, I thought about asking him to Christmas dinner.

Dumb idea, I decided a minute later. He had a family somewhere, and friends. Besides, he'd think we were all crazy. Heck, we were all crazy. I realized that every time we got together. And I loved it.

Why *did* I stay away so long between visits?

Because I had a life, another whole life, and it wasn't situated in Connor Falls, Pennsylvania.

With a sigh, I stopped dancing and started

peeling. The peeler whispered over each potato, skins curling from the utensil to plop into the sink. I realized with a start I could hear them slithering over each other onto the stainless steel. Mom had turned the music off. I glanced aside at her.

"Honey," she said, clutching a half a dozen carrots in each hand, "what's wrong?"

"What? Nothing, Mom. What makes you think something is wrong?"

"Your face," she said. "Do you not realize how transparent you are?"

I turned back to my task, blinking desperately and rapidly.

"And the tears," she added. "That's a pretty big clue, too."

Stupid face, stupid tears, stupid whatever this was making me cry like a baby. I dropped the peeler into the sink and dashed first one hand, then the other, across my eyes, filling my nostrils with the scent from raw potatoes. I heard the carrots clunk on the tabletop. A second later Mom's arms went around me, making me cry harder still.

"What's going on here?"

Beyond Mom's shoulder, Dad stood in the

doorway, his brows arching up toward his hairline, which was a feat. He'd really gotten quite bald in the front.

"Nothing," I said, stepping from Mom's embrace, pulling my sleeve over my fingers to scrub at my eyes again. "I don't know."

"Oh. Well maybe I should just step outside, give you a minute."

Mom snorted. "I think our daughter's feeling a bit homesick, that's all," she said, sneaking past me to take over the peeling. "What are you doing home so early?"

He shot me a crooked grin, whipping two small floral bouquets from behind him, each one wrapped in holiday-patterned paper and likely picked up from the grocery store on his way home. "I just figured I'd spend a little extra time with my homesick daughter before dinner, and to give you both these."

* * *

Later, when the house went quiet, I snuck out.

Bundled in my coat and boots and scarf, I crept across the porch, crossed the driveway and walked slowly into the fields beyond. My breath frosted in

the air. Overhead, stars glittered hard and bright in the dark night sky. Far across the open field white-yellow eyes glowed as several deer watched me, gauging my intent, my direction. I kept walking, not toward them, but in a wide arc around the house, heading toward the area where Mom planted all her flowers and vegetables. A few pumpkins had withered on the vines, but I managed to spot their humped signatures in the shadows before I fell over them.

I shoved my hands down into my pockets, reassured by the hard edge from my cell phone burrowed deep in the right. I didn't anticipate any need for it, and once upon a time no one had little phones constantly on their person, but if I happened to miss a pumpkin or just a furrow in the ground, I could find myself glad to be so indoctrinated. Stuff happened. Stuff like slipping on the ice and fracturing an elbow (a long time ago, thank goodness). Stuff like car accidents which left a person in a condition I couldn't quite fathom. One day I might acquire a fuller understanding, but probably not. Christmas was a-coming. The day after that I'd be driving home.

However, he did perform freelance work for Mom on a pretty regular basis, I'd been told. When I came to visit we'd meet again, and maybe sooner rather than later, because Mom was right. Her daughter was feeling a little homesick. More than a little. How odd. At least I told myself it was odd. Maybe it wasn't. Maybe it really, really wasn't.

I kept walking, past the raised beds that would in warmer weather house all the cutting flowers, along the pathways where vegetable plants would grow to either side, around the gleaming hulk of the greenhouse erected over the summer. Mom had pointed it out to me through the window, thrilled with the practical addition. She would start her seedlings in it, rather than filling the back porch with them. She also intended to force paper white and narcissus bulbs and grow poinsettias for sale next fall. Always planning was Mom.

Always.

After the wedding and reception on Saturday, I figured she'd get down to Christmas preparation in earnest. Not everything could be performed months in advance, no matter how carefully a body planned. Some things had to be last minute. Like baking

dozens and dozens of cookies, packing them into tins for family members, friends, gifts and donations. The Christmas after they'd moved into Hummingbird Farm Mom and Dad started purchasing balled trees for inside the house, planting them in another field out back after the holidays. Mom liked to have three of them, one in the huge kitchen, one in the living room, one on the front porch. The trees were already in place, but one hadn't been decorated yet. I liked that part, breaking out the old boxes, looking through the ornaments, hanging each one and the lights. As for dinner, Dad always made the turkey. Roasting the turkey was his specialty. Simon made bread, usually delicious bread. Occasionally I'd make a pie. My success in the pie-baking arena had been so sporadic I often pretended I forgot and would run out for a store-bought one.

Every year I looked forward to these last-minute things. They, and family, were what made the holidays special.

I started shuffling my rubber soles through the fallen leaves while I walked, the crisp sounds trailing after me, echoing off the greenhouse. An owl hooted nearby, answered by another in the distant woods. I

did miss Connor Falls. I truly did, but it wasn't my home anymore, no matter how much it felt like it when I came back. What was I supposed to do with those feelings? What good did they serve? In a practical world, home was where your job took you. In an emotional one, home was where your heart resided. Very rarely did the two meet. In my parent's world they had.

Some nocturnal creature darted through the leaves. Once my heart rhythm returned to normal, I headed around to the front porch and quietly let myself back inside. I made my way to the kitchen, turned on the light over the stove. Shirking my coat off, I draped it over a chair back along with my scarf and set about warming up milk in a pan. People, people like me, always dismissed simple remedies and opted for staring at the television all night hoping to drop off again. Or took a walk in the cold and the dark with the very thoughts keeping them awake coming to full light in their heads, blood pumping furiously through a chilled body, because yeah, that would knock a person out. Mom believed in the whole drink your warm milk thing. It worked when we were kids, back when we trusted everything as

truth. It might work now.

"Can't sleep?"

The spoon in my hand flew through the air and clattered on the floor.

"Mom! Jeez, get a bell."

She came in, eyed my coat, sat in the chair next to it. "Been out rambling, have you?"

We wore nearly identical sleep attire, Mom and I. Ratty old sweat pants and a heavy, seen-better-days tee shirt. Maybe I'd become her one day, morph right into my mother. I could do worse, I knew.

I scooped up the spoon, rinsed it and gave the pot's contents a stir. "Want some?" I offered, reaching for the container I hadn't yet put away.

"Sure."

After tipping more milk into the pot, I took two mugs from the cabinet and set them side by side on the counter, fidgeting in a compulsive way with the handles until they were lined up.

"Want to tell me what's on your mind?" Mom asked.

Not really, I thought.

"You don't have to, you know," she added, as if I'd spoken.

"I'm just working through some stuff, Mom." Stir, stir, stir. I lifted the spoon to the light, checking for steam. Satisfied the milk had heated through I filled the mugs and carried them to the table, setting Mom's before her. I picked mine back up, went to the small alcove where the counter and cabinets ended, and shimmied myself into the deep window sill. If I'd grown up here, this would have been my favorite place, a cozy, not-quite hideaway near enough to the fireplace to see the flames, feel its heat. Even now, the embers glowing in the ashes from the earlier fire emitted warmth.

"What kind of stuff?" she asked, taking a tentative sip from the cup held in both hands.

"Life stuff. The kind of stuff life throws at you. Things you have to work your way through, make up your mind about, maybe even change."

"That never stops."

"I know."

Mom set her mug down, fingers clasped and interlocked around it. "What would you change?"

I sighed, leaning my head back against the cold window glass. "Maybe everything."

Wow. I couldn't believe I'd said that out loud. I

swallowed a quick hit of milk, followed by another. Mom watched me from across the room. The stove light highlighted the lovely silver in her hair.

"You can't change everything," she said, stating what I knew to be the obvious. "What's most important to you? That's what you work on first." She lifted the mug to her mouth again.

"Aren't I too young for a mid-life crisis?"

And clunked it back onto the table, choking on the milk she'd been swallowing. I started to get up from the window sill. She waved me back.

"I'm fine," she said, wiping her chin with the back of her hand. "It's not a crisis, Suze. It's recognition. I say it's never too early for that. Or too late."

She finished her calcium sedative and went back to bed shortly after, leaving me with the washing up, as was fitting. I'd made the mess.

*   *   *

I woke up with the winter sun beating through the parted curtains onto my face. That, and someone pounding on the door. I thought I might have imagined the second part, but when it repeated along

with a young voice calling my name, I tossed back the covers and leapt from the bed in a race to the door.

"What?" I shouted as I yanked it open.

Seven-year-old Stuart stood on the other side, totally unperturbed by the fact his aunt had just yelled at him. He grinned at me and gave me a saucy little salute, right hand to brow.

"Don't you have school?" I asked.

"Not today."

I stared at him, waiting.

"Gran needs you. She says get up."

"Is she hurt, leg broken, anything like that?"

"No."

"Good," I said. "I'll be down as soon as I get dressed."

"Better hurry. There's a lady in the living room and she's crying an awful lot."

Fully clothed in two minutes flat, I hurried toward the living room, combing my hair with my fingers. I could hear the snuffling and stuttering words my entire trek down the stairs. I heard them still as I rounded the corner, punctuated by Mom patiently trying to soothe. When I entered the room, I

saw a stranger who looked to be younger than me perched on the ottoman's edge, head in her hands, shaking it as she continued her nearly unintelligible communication. Mom sat on the couch, patting the woman's back distractedly. She looked up as I crossed the floor, staring with some unknown intent at me over the woman's head.

The bride? I mouthed. She nodded.

I went straight up to them both, fitted my hand against Mom's back and pulled her up from the sofa. I propelled her lightly away and took her place.

"Wait," said the bride, her reddened eyes following my mother's movements. "Where are you going?"

"My mom's going to make us some tea," I said. "We'll pretend we're in England where tea soothes all wounds."

"Y-your mom?" she stammered, gaze on me now, searching my face as Mom made a hasty exit.

"Yes. I'm Susan. What's your name?"

"C-Carla. She's making us tea, you said?"

"Yep. In the meantime, why don't you tell me what's wrong? Why are you upset?" This woman's wedding reception was supposed to be taking place

here tomorrow. Only one reason for being so distressed came to mind.

She scrubbed her eyes with the heel of her palm, smearing mascara. High color splotched her cheeks. "I only want it to be perfect. That's what I've always dreamed I'd have—a perfect wedding."

I took a deep breath, recalling my silly childhood dreams for a winter wedding. Eventually you outgrew such nonsense, or at least came to realize perfection wouldn't be found in the wedding, but in the reasons for it.

"Why do you think it won't be exactly what you wanted?" I asked. Please, I begged silently, don't say it's because he dumped you. There'd be no coming back from that.

She didn't. She shifted on the ottoman, smoothed the skirt she wore. "I don't know. I keep second-guessing myself. I'm sure I've been driving your mother crazy. I'm just afraid that…that when the time comes, he'll be so disappointed."

"He? Your fiancé, you mean?"

She nodded.

"Disappointed in what? The reception?"

Again, the nod, her lavender bangs falling into

her eyes, catching in her damp lashes.

"Did he have any input in the planning?"

"Yes," she whispered.

"Has he made any complaints?"

She shook her head.

"Does he love you?"

Her eyes flew wide. "Yes, he does. We love each other very much."

I straightened, pulled away slightly, adopting a no-nonsense manner. "Then I don't quite understand all the stress about perfection. You love each other. That's all that matters, right? Nothing in this life is ever going to be perfect. You're marrying a man you love and who loves you back, so I think the plan would be to always face those imperfections together, yes? Make the best of them."

She stared at me for a few moments in silence. I caught a glimpse of Mom in the hall. She stepped back from view.

"Okay," Carla said. "Okay."

"Come on, let's go outside and walk through this, so you can see it in your head without all the worrying. I'll tell Mom to skip the tea. She'll have to come with us because, really, I don't know the first

thing about event planning and what you guys have cooked up. Sound good?"

"Yes, please," said Carla, rising with a watery smile from the cushioned ottoman. She snatched her coat off the couch and put it back on, shoving her arms in the sleeves. "Will you be there? Tomorrow, I mean. I know your mom will be. She said she always is, to make sure things run smoothly. But will you be there, too?"

"Of course, she will," Mom said from the doorway. She waved a hand for us to follow. "Carla, you're going to have a great day."

Together, we went through the converted barn and the details of Carla's reception, from décor to music, seating to menu, and all the mini-events to take place within. I had seen Mom's brochures, which explained her dream and the humble beginnings of Hummingbird Farm before outlining everything available on the property and in the fabulous, eclectic venue. I had a feeling Carla hadn't read the brochure, because when Mom launched into her heart's journey, Carla listened with utter fascination. Afterward, she threw her arms around my mother and hugged her.

"Thank you so much. I'm sorry for being such a pain," she said.

Mom dismissed the apology as unnecessary. "We all get jitters over something. I'll see you tomorrow, Carla. I'm looking forward to it."

"Me, too." Carla giggled, tears long gone. She fluttered to her car like a butterfly, relieved and happy. Mom pulled the barn doors closed, locked them. She turned to me.

"Thank you," she said.

"Ah, it was nothing…short of a miracle." I laughed. She didn't.

"I'm serious, Suze. This is what you do. Talk to people. It's a gift."

We started walking back toward the house. "Well, I did go to school for it. Let's not dismiss all the money spent."

"No degree gives you what comes to you naturally. You've always had it, even when you were little. You talked, people listened. It's your tone, your demeanor, the things you say."

Inside, I experienced a quiet, fizzing joy. Outside, I shrugged. Mom touched my hand, squeezed, let go.

"There's something I'd like to do, Mom," I said.

"What's that?"

We mounted the porch steps, crossed to the door. I stood for the briefest moment staring at the screen, at a delicate milkweed seed trapped in the mesh. I let out my breath. "I want to invite Arlo to Christmas dinner."

"I already did," said Mom. She smiled at me in an odd, gentle way and went inside.

Chapter Four

"You'll do what?"

I gazed at Mom across the breakfast table. Dad sat opposite her and opposite me sat young Stuart, his head turning from me to Mom and back again. I had no idea why he'd spent the night without his brother. Maybe so he could beat me at checkers nine out of twelve games,

or maybe because he knew his grandmother would prepare his favorite pancakes for breakfast. Before bed, he'd also cajoled me into agreeing to a walk in the fields with him first thing. We'd already accomplished our trek, watching the sun rise. I'd pay for that later, I knew. It was going to be a long day.

"I'll tend the bar," I repeated, "with whoever you've hired." I'd helped pay my expenses in college by bartending. I didn't want to be at Carla's wedding as a guest, or even on the sidelines in a semi-managerial position. I wanted something I could concentrate on, to keep me busy and diverted from the crowd. I'd never been good at parties, always the one who opted to hover near the door or do the washing up, repeatedly, throughout the night.

Mom blew a breath from her nose. "Fine. You'll have to wear the uniform, then."

"White shirt, black pants? Not a problem."

Recognizing the crisis had been averted, Stuart returned his attention to his pancakes. Dad winked at me over his coffee mug. He'd never been one for crowds either. Dad understood.

"Arthur," Mom addressed him, "would you mind clearing away the breakfast mess? Lots to do, little time."

He smiled at her and then set his wink on Stuart, who broke out into giggles.

"Suze?" she said to me. "Coming?"

I hadn't exactly volunteered for the morning setup, but I could see Mom wanted me to join her. I didn't mind. Simon was out there already, as well as two guys in their early twenties she kept "on-call" for the job.

"I brought the wagon around last night," she told me as I followed her out to the porch. "We'll load the centerpieces into it and bring them over, get the tablecloths on, make sure those boys have gotten the chairs where they belong, and, well, you know the drill."

I did. Whenever I was around and an event had been scheduled, I lent a hand. Why not? It helped Mom and Dad and allowed us all to have more time together. If I went my own way instead, I'd never see Mom on those weekends.

Once the tables were topped with cloth and tableware, tiny lights in hurricane jars were lowered into the middle of each centerpiece and extra lights hung above to add to the fairytale Christmas atmosphere. More plants were brought in, the bar wiped and cleaned and stocked. Wreaths adorned the walls. The caterers arrived in the midst of the minor

chaos, setting themselves up in the kitchen at the barn's back end. Locating the vacuum, I engaged in constant battle with the leaves being tracked in. Finally, only the caterers were left, chattering away at a distance, confined for now to their work in the kitchen. They supplied the wait staff, too, which would be arriving about a half hour before the guests. Simon had retrieved his youngest and gone home. Mom and I stood in the middle of the floor alone.

"What's next?" I asked.

"Grab the seating chart. We'll put out name tags and the favors. The DJ will be here about two hours before the reception starts and he'll get the sound system set. I have no idea how to do that and no desire to learn."

"There's something in this world you don't want to conquer? I'm ashamed to be your daughter."

She shot me a withering glance before pivoting full circle on her heel for another look around.

"Everything is beautiful," I assured her. "Carla and her new hubby will be thrilled."

Mom nodded, lips compressed. She opened them to speak, closed them again.

"What?" I said.

"Are you sure you want to bartend? When Carla

asked you to be here, I pictured us together, somehow, working the room."

"Working the room? Mom, you make us sound like comedians."

She sighed, closed her eyes, opened them.

"Obviously you don't find me as amusing as you once did," I added, "so no standup routine for me, I guess."

"Susan."

The diminutive of my name had fallen by the wayside. Manipulation hovered in the offing. Oh, to be a child again and not resent being stage-managed by my mother. Oh, wait, I did then, too. Probably more so. Now, for the most part I merely shrugged it off and moved on.

"Mom, if you want something, please just ask me, okay? I'm assuming us doing this together today means a lot to you. Mom? Say yes or no."

Her mouth quivered, seeming to struggle to hold back a smile. "Yes."

"Okay, then. I'll see if I brought something halfway decent to wear."

"Thank you."

"You owe me."

"I birthed and raised you," she said. "I think I win

this round."

"Yeah," I agreed, "you do."

I had a nice dress in my suitcase I hadn't gotten around to hanging up yet. Leaving Mom to speak with the caterers about some issue, I hurried to the house to yank the garment out and hang it in the bathroom for a little steam therapy while I showered. Passing the upstairs den, I spotted my dad watching television, slouched into the heavily cushioned sofa with his legs crossed at the ankle and propped up on the coffee table.

I skidded to a halt, leaning into the room. "Not that you don't deserve it, but how can you be so relaxed with everything going on?"

"Your mom tells me I have to be," he said. "And far be it from me to disobey her orders." He grinned.

Dad had retired the year before from the job he'd held for twenty-five years, but still worked two to three days a week as a consultant. Mom liked to see him relax, and I certainly didn't begrudge him the opportunity. It surprised me he could, though, with Mom going full-bore.

"What are you watching?"

He glanced at the flat screen hanging on the wall opposite. "I have no idea."

I nodded. "Best way to relax. Don't get invested."

I started again down the hallway. He called me back. Sticking my head around the doorframe, I smiled at him.

"Yeah, Dad?"

He rose from the couch, walked over and placed his hand on my shoulder, a large hand lying gently. "It's good to have you home."

"It's good to be here," I said.

"You mean that, don't you?"

"Of course I do."

"We miss you when you're not here."

I blinked back tears, unable to respond. I took his hand from my shoulder, squeezed it.

"Honey," he said, "are you sure you're okay?"

I nodded. "I will be. I have some stuff I have to work through, and I'm avoiding it."

"Can I help?"

I looked up into his face, the face Simon's would surely become in later years. "You already have."

I left him standing there gazing after me, the way he used to if he happened to be around when I headed out on a date or an evening with my friends. At the bedroom door I glanced back, caught a glimpse of him watching me still. I recognized his concern, his love, and then he turned away.

I didn't want him to waste his whole day worrying about me. I would work things out. I always did.

Digging through my suitcase, I found the dress rumpled at the bottom. Not exactly wedding material, but a sleek-fitting little black dress always served its purpose. I'd brought two sweaters with me to wear with it, having been unable to make up my mind. The one was definitely in the running for our annual ugly Christmas sweater competition, but the other, lightweight, gray and mid-thigh length, would provide a much more sophisticated effect. I located a hanger and slipped the dress onto it. The material was such that most wrinkles fell right out from gravity. I figured I'd leave it hanging by the window for a bit instead of the bathroom and let the sun through the glass warm up the fabric. Perhaps I wouldn't need to do anything with the garment except put it on.

I hadn't accounted for how tall these old farmhouse windows were. In order to reach the curtain rod, I climbed onto a chair and then stepped onto the deep sill. I still had to stretch to hook the hanger onto the rod above the frame. Was I that short? Really?

Balanced in the window, I took several minutes to enjoy the view. Beyond the fields gray woods dotted with evergreen marched up the nearest hill. At night the

pinprick lights from a house perched at the top would glow. By day the house remained hidden, no matter the season. The road out front continued past the hill into Connor Falls proper. To the left, more hills lay like plumped muted pillows. In spring and summer they would be greener than green and in autumn filled with color. I'd grown up in this beautiful area. I missed it.

Through the glass I heard gravel crunching and leaned close to peer to my right, toward the visible family parking spaces. I watched Arlo's black Jeep pull in and park, spied him behind the wheel by squashing my cheek flat against the glass. He sat a moment, head bowed, his fingertips pressed to his brow. After a few seconds he lifted his head, stared out across the fields. He got out, pushed the door closed, and with his hand touching the vehicle every few inches, made his way to the grassy area in front of it.

I saw him clearly now, hunched against the cold in his suit jacket. He had his head up, his eyes steady on a horizon, his dark hair blowing crazily around his face in a sudden breeze that whipped his jacket back, too. The expression on his profiled features remained impassive in the manner I now recognized as intense concentration. He'd told me about the need for it, in the ten minutes we'd remained on the sidewalk outside his

house before he'd said goodbye and gone in. He said he was better, so much better than he had been, but he still had to spend some time orienting himself whenever he exited a moving vehicle, waiting for the sensation like his brain rolling away to end. He had to focus hard, too, when walking from point A to point B. He still searched for words that used to come to him without any conscious thought, but it was better, he said, than not being able to remember them at all.

Watching him from the window, I understood what he meant about the injuries a person couldn't see. Not being able to focus on a cast, a limp, a physical scar, made it extremely difficult for a person to understand the injury's extent from the outside. He'd done a lot of talking in those ten minutes, Arlo had, haltingly, weighing vocabulary to construct into sentences, me in silence, just listening. I couldn't imagine how I would feel, no longer possessing an ease of function in my everyday environment. I'd said as much to him. He hadn't answered. He thought I felt sorry for him, I could tell. I didn't feel sorry for him. I felt humbled to know a person fighting so hard to get their life back. We all did it. We all fought for something. That didn't make his journey any less important or any less impressive, and it sure as heck impressed me.

Down in the yard, Arlo turned his head. Not quickly. He couldn't do quickly. Even so, I reacted as if he could, as if he might catch me spying on him, and I took a hasty step back. Right off the sill. I landed with a crash, but unharmed, on the carpeted floor. I'd barely caught my breath before a fist pounded on the door.

"Suze! Are you all right?"

"I'm fine, Dad," I called out. "Dropped my suitcase off the bed. Sorry if I scared you."

"That sounded pretty darned heavy for a suitcase," he said. "You're sure you're okay?"

I righted myself and scurried to the door, cracking it open, smiling out at him and hoping my embarrassment wouldn't show. "I'm good, Dad. See? All in one piece."

"Well, if you say so."

"I do," I said. "Go back to relaxing. And thanks for checking."

With a grunted reply, he returned to the den. I shut the door, went back to the window. The lawn was empty. Arlo had gone.

*   *   *

Mom gave my attire, my entire person, an

approving nod. "Those earrings are cute. Didn't you give me a pair like them?"

I fingered the tiny, festive wreaths on my lobes. "I did. Maybe you could wear them today. We'd at least fit it with Carla's wedding theme."

"Good idea," she agreed. Turning on her heel, she hurried up the stairs, presumably to get them. The wedding party would be arriving shortly for photos. The DJ had set up, the wait staff was receiving last minute instructions from the caterers, and Arlo had temporarily joined Dad in the den. We'd crossed paths in the upstairs hallway. Arlo had given me a swift hello, his eyes not on my feet, but on the dress I wore. I supposed that was progress.

Mom returned, affixing the earrings into her ears. She looked gorgeous in a fabulously understated, sophisticated way. The earrings might have detracted a bit from the effect, but I knew Mom wouldn't care.

"So, what do I have to do?" I asked her. "What are my duties as your sidekick?" This was another reason I had wanted to bartend. I preferred a specific function in a situation where strangers abounded, rather than being responsible for making small talk beyond what-are-you-having. Mom didn't know that, or if she did, she probably considered my introverted nature something I needed to get over. The ability to talk to people and have them listen to me didn't mean I had a talent for conversing with everyone willy-nilly.

She and I started out the door, but not before Mom called up to Arlo, letting him know she'd spotted the limo with the bridal party maneuvering into the drive. The first photos were to be taken around and inside the gazebo, a lovely white-washed structure that had been planted beside the barn and surrounded by a small garden pretty much solely with event photography in mind. For this occasion, it had been decorated yesterday with greens and poinsettias and twinkling lights, per the bride's request. I hesitated on the porch, watching the limo pull up across several event parking spaces. Mom went on ahead, somehow managing to appear both friendly and business-like. I took a deep breath. The door opened behind me. A step on the floorboards vibrated beneath my comfortable yet dressy flats.

Not Dad. He stomped as if warning all the earth's little critters out of his way. Stomped like a giant, even though he didn't possess a giant's girth. Tall, yes, but like Simon, a good wind might topple him.

"Steady on," said Arlo. "They won't bite."

I turned to make certain he spoke to me and not

himself, because I figured those words could work for me or him. "I hope not," I said. "I'm probably past due for a tetanus booster."

He laughed out loud. I liked his laugh, liked the charming, contagious sound of it. I fought to keep a straight face, but in the end I gave in.

"Stupid joke," I said. "Thanks for laughing."

His eyes met mine, slipped away. Suddenly he looked down, reaching into his pocket. He pulled out two small objects, separated them and fitted one into each ear. I tipped my head for a better look. They appeared to be soft, flesh-colored earplugs.

"Those help?" I asked.

He nodded. "Too many conversations. Plus loud noise." He shrugged, lifted his finger and wiggled the plug in his left ear.

"Got any extras?"

"Afraid not," he said, "but I'll bring some next time."

He didn't ask why I wanted them. Quite honestly, I didn't know either, except I envisioned dampening down the noise could be quite soothing. I didn't need a head injury to find a wedding reception's bombardment overwhelming.

I also didn't ask about the *next time*, about the two

words thrown out there, hinting at a promise or a hope—or merely uttered without thought. After all, he would be here at the next event requiring a photographer, whereas I had apparently fallen into the habit of staying away for six months at a time. A habit I wanted to break. A habit I wanted to more than break.

We descended the stairs side by side and crossed the lot. I asked him if he needed any assistance setting up equipment or lighting, but he assured me he had it under control. I asked him if he'd always done photography for a living, or if he'd done something different before. I didn't have to say before what. The accident had been a defining moment in his life.

He shook his head. "It used to be a hobby. Even— eventually I found I could still do that. My old job? I didn't go back."

He said nothing else. I kept my curiosity to myself. Inside the barn we went our separate ways, he to my mother's side to address the pending photos, and me to a corner, standing in the shadow of a tall, realistic fake evergreen decked out in clear lights. I rearranged the ones nearest to me. Mom caught my eye, made a face and a quick hand movement. I ceased toying with the bulbs and went over to where she stood.

Carla, who had been conferring with her

bridesmaids, turned her head and spotted me. She hustled over with crisp, sliding satin noises. A man I presumed to be her husband stood on the sidelines next to another tuxedoed guy. He appeared patiently amused by the proceedings.

"Susan!" Carla hugged me as best she could accomplish, given the gown's massive volume. She stepped back. "I love your earrings! Your mom has the same ones on."

"Festive, right?" I touched the jewelry at my lobes. "You look beautiful."

Grinning, she twirled on the spot. Behind her, the bridesmaids in their silver-sashed, celery-green gowns eyed us with a mere half second of curiosity before turning a collective gaze on Arlo. Speculation showed itself in each unguarded expression. Naturally, being a wedding, they would check him out that way. Weddings were notorious for hookups or for the conjecture about hopeful eventualities. Something interesting existed about the person of Arlo Woods, for sure. I'd been trying hard not to notice it.

He looked up from wherever his concentration had taken him, straight into my eyes. He smiled. My breath rushed out. Before I could smile back, he returned his attention to my mother. I noted how still my mother

stood when speaking to him and how he managed to keep his focus on her face. I, on the other hand, was always quite animated around him, what with random head movements and the constant repositioning of body parts. Therein, I realized, might lie the problem. I reminded myself to be more tranquil next time we spoke.

"The photographer," began Carla, turning to me. "What's his name again?"

"Arlo," I said.

"Yes, right, Arlo. He's really good. Your mom said he was, but I didn't quite believe her until I saw samples. I'm afraid I still gave her a hard time. I just…well, you know."

"I know."

"Is there something wrong with him?"

I straightened my spine. "What do you mean?"

"Is he slow or something?"

I knew what she implied. And like my mother and brother before me, I knew his story wasn't mine to tell. Instead, I said, "He's deliberate in his actions. He has to be. Does that matter?"

"Oh, no," she said, "not at all. I only asked because I didn't know if I had to be careful in any way, so I wouldn't unintentionally upset him."

I cocked my head to the side, studying her profile. She'd asked out of kindness, not condemnation or ridicule. "He had an accident," I said. "He's getting better every day. Please don't tell him I told you. Please don't mention it at all."

She nodded. "I won't."

Mom called them all over. Dresses were lifted from the ground, hands clutched bouquets, tux sleeves were smoothed. They all followed Arlo and Mom outside. The gazebo's positioning was such that the sturdy red barn protected it and its occupants from the wind's usual direction. Left to my own devices, I strolled around double-checking place settings, smoothing tablecloths, chatted a bit with the DJ when he came out from the men's room, made sure he had the opening music list, spoke with the wait staff hovering near the kitchen door. Finally, I went out to witness Arlo and my mom in action.

They worked well together. He asked her opinion and she respected his. Mom shuffled the party around at his direction like pieces on a chessboard and the camera clicked away. Arlo staged faux candid as well as dramatic and formal poses. He moved in for close ups and even used a macro lens for what would undoubtedly prove to be a striking photo of the rings on

the bride and groom's interlocked fingers. Afterward, Mom escorted the party to a lounge area to await the guests' arrival. Arlo and I were left by the gazebo alone.

"You should go inside," he said without looking at me. "You're cold."

"What makes you think that?"

"You're shivering."

I watched him gather up the equipment he'd brought outside with him, systematically packing up what he'd only have to unpack again inside. His actions revealed a careful routine designed to prevent, I realized, his forgetting.

I didn't speak again until he'd finished. "Why did you move to Connor Falls, Arlo?"

He glanced at me and away, settling his gaze on the solid, level lines of the barn. He slung his camera bag over his shoulder. "I used to visit my grandparents here. I liked it then. I like it now."

I fell in beside him when he started moving. "I didn't realize you had a connection to the area. Do your grandparents still live here? Oh, stupid question. You said 'used to'."

"They moved to…" He paused and squeezed his eyes shut, then opened them. "Arizona. My folks, too. I

don't see them all as much as I'd like."

"Me either," I surprised myself by admitting. "And I don't live anywhere near that far away."

He stopped by the door, put his hand on the wall and turned to face me. "Why did you leave Connor Falls?"

I bit my lip, sucked in a long breath through my nose. "Long story."

"You'll tell me sometime?"

"Sure," I said. "I absolutely will."

Chapter Five

I kept an eye on Arlo. Not because I thought he needed me to, or that he required any help. He wouldn't have tolerated that, I'm sure. I suspected he'd been treated as though he did, folks jumping to conclusions, thinking he was in some way weaker or lesser equipped than they, not recognizing the hidden strength he likely had to summon up to make it through the day. The

impulses in our brains controlled everything we did, didn't they? What an extraordinary mess that would be, if our brains went awry.

I kept an eye on Arlo because I couldn't help myself. I observed him working his way through the crowd with the camera, pausing every now and then to get his bearings. Framing the shots, clicking away, every step made in awareness to where he placed his feet, to his surroundings. It had to be exhausting. It exhausted me to watch and yet I couldn't look away. He caught me at it, more than once. I had no idea what he thought about my unintended surveillance. Occasionally he smiled. More often than not he turned back to his job without acknowledgment.

Mom caught me doing it, too, when she had to ask me three times to fetch a corkscrew from the house because the one belonging to the caterers had broken and they'd been unable to locate another in the barn kitchen.

"What on earth are you looking at, Suze?" And then she saw. "Oh." The single syllable expanded like a bubble around us, filled with a kind of semi-silence pushing the clamor from the reception away. She stared at me, her expression unreadable until her lips formed a slow curve.

"The corkscrew in the house, Suze," she said, eyebrows lifting. "Can you get it?"

"Corkscrew. Yes. Right."

I hurried from the barn, grateful for the flat shoes on my feet. I scampered across the driveway, up the steps, across the porch, not stopping until I reached the kitchen. My cheeks burned. From the cold, I told myself. I could do that sometimes, lie outright to myself, recognize the falsehood and still insist on it silently in my head.

Scrabbling through the drawers, I searched for the implement. From upstairs I heard the television and a sound I recognized as Dad's snoring. The old farmhouse felt comfortable, welcoming, embracing somehow. I'd never wondered why Mom and Dad had bought it. I wouldn't have hesitated either. The house possessed good vibes. So much so, I stood for a few minutes longer in the kitchen, found corkscrew in hand, and attempted to absorb a little more of them into my reeling senses.

I had to admit I wasn't watching Arlo only because I admired his determination, or because he had that certain windblown appearance to him which always caught my eye, or because I recognized and empathized with a bruised soul refusing to wither. Mom knew.

Mom *knew*. She knew I liked him, liked him already, this man I hadn't even heard of three days ago, this man whose presence in my mind I couldn't allow to influence my decision-making. I'd expected to come home this Christmas, the season for hope and promise and forgiveness and love, to sort things out in a quiet space away from my own.

My first mistake had been thinking it would be quiet. There was a wedding going on sixty feet away for crying out loud.

A wedding needing the corkscrew. Focus Susan Hayley Hardwick. Focus.

By the time I returned, Mom had borrowed one from a guest who apparently carried a multi-tool in his pocket wherever he went and however he dressed. She still appeared relieved to find I'd brought a better one, or perhaps merely that I'd come back. According to the schedule I'd previously viewed, the wedding cake would soon be brought out stimulating the ensuing photo op, followed by the whole garter thing while the cake was cut up for serving. Carla wanted to hold off tossing the bouquet until she and Steve were ready to depart. They had a late plane to catch, so it couldn't be much longer, leaving the guests free to dance the evening away after they'd gone. The bar would close

and coffee would be served in massive quantities to assure safe driving at the appropriate hour. With effort, I avoided checking the time on my watch every five minutes. With a stronger effort, I forced my gaze not to drift after Arlo.

Someone bumped against me. I turned to find the bride at my elbow, all her pearly whites showing in earnest.

"Carla," I said.

"Everybody's having a great time."

"Of course they are. Are you?"

She nodded.

"Steve?"

"Yep," she said. "It's just like you said."

"Don't sweat the small stuff and all that?"

"Yes." She wriggled from side to side in time to the music. She'd cast aside her veil at some point. Her short lavender hair stuck out in places it probably wasn't meant to. "This is the perfect time of year to get married. Not June."

"I used to think I'd like a winter wedding, too."

Her smile dropped. "Used to?"

"Well," I said, "when I was younger and wanted to get married someday, I thought it would be a magical season for one."

Frowning in consideration, Carla pivoted her hand back and forth, the liquid in the glass she held sloshing up at the sides. "And you don't want to now? Get married someday, I mean."

"It would be nice to love and be loved first. After all, arranged marriages are so last year."

She burst out laughing. I managed to rescue the glass from her fist before whatever it contained ended up on her gown.

"You're so funny," she gasped. "I like you."

"I like you, too, Carla," I said, sniffing at the glass I cupped in my hand.

"He does, too."

"Steve? That's nice. I try not to be totally disagreeable, if I can help it."

She snorted back a guffaw, wiping at her eyes with her fingertips. "I don't mean Steve," she said, "although I think he does. I bet he does. I'm sure he does."

I waited, struggling to keep a straight face.

"I'm talking about the photographer."

I blinked, fully aware of my dramatically sweeping lashes. "Arlo?"

"There's only the one," she said.

I wanted to ask how she knew this, and at the same

time I didn't. I wasn't standing next to Betsy Gruber at junior prom, agonizing over Robby Smith's affections or lack thereof.

"Whenever you disappeared for a minute, I'd see him glancing around for you," Carla went on. "And when you left the building a little while ago? He asked your mom if you were all right."

"That doesn't mean anything," I started to argue, but she smirked and took back her glass, giving me a long, knowing, somewhat inebriated look before she suddenly waved to someone and hurried off.

Mom appeared at my side. "Carla looks happy," she said.

"Yeah," I said, "but don't put too much stock in it. She's also delusional."

*   *   *

I missed the bouquet. Deliberately, in fact. Mom had pushed me into the fray when all the single ladies were called upon to trust their future hopes to the ball-catching abilities they may or may not have garnered as children. I stood with my hands folded together at my waist. Just because I was in the crowd didn't mean I had to play. Unfortunately, the fragrant, over-sized posy landed within inches of my feet. I stared at the fallen blooms while all the women who'd missed their chance at the prize stared at me. After a momentary indecisiveness, I snatched the bouquet from the floor.

"Goodness," I said, "we've never had this happen before. Carla? Shall we give it another go?"

Carla agreed. I returned the bouquet to her and slipped from the group, almost bumping into Arlo, who stood at the ready, camera in hand.

"You didn't get a shot of that, did you?" I asked in an undertone close to his ear so he could hear me through the plug. He smelled good, like an herbal soap.

"I'll remember to delete it," he said, raising the camera to his eye. "I promise."

"I'll hold you to it."

As the night would soon be winding down, I went over to the bar and asked for a wine spritzer. The bartender handed me the twelve-ounce bottle, opened, and a glass. I slid the glass back at him with my forefinger and a smile. "I'm good," I said. A yell on the floor indicated someone's success with the bouquet. I knew her, the girl who'd caught it. I used to babysit her. I took a dainty swig from the spritzer bottle, feeling older than I had when I walked into the reception three hours earlier.

Mom strolled over. She jerked her head toward the girl still jumping up and down on her toes, the bouquet

plastered to her chest. "Didn't you babysit her at some point?"

"Yeah, I did." I handed her my bottle for a sip. She took it, looking straight into my eyes with an expression I couldn't misinterpret. "We're not getting any younger," I added.

"Shut up." She laughed, a small, short sound, and drank down half the contents. Afterward, she coughed and wiped her hand across her mouth. "What is that? I thought it was some kind of fancy water."

"Sorry. A blackberry wine spritzer."

"Ah, okay." She turned her head to perform a crowd-check. "Why are you drinking?"

"I was in the mood. Besides, they're not that strong."

"Not unless you slug down half a bottle in one go, I expect."

"Yes, there's always that. You going to be okay?"

"Always," she said and walked away to see the bride and groom out the door to the returned limo.

I slowly finished the spritzer, since I really wasn't sure about the alcohol content. I'd always assumed on the occasion I'd had one that it wasn't quite the same as, say, a glass filled with bourbon, but what did I know. In the present environment and as an unofficial

representative of a Hummingbird Farm event, I needed to keep my wits about me.

Ninety minutes following the newlyweds' unconventional early departure less than a dozen couples remained on the dance floor, no longer in sweaty, disheveled gyration, but embraced and moving to slower, quieter tunes. The other guests were seated at tables enjoying coffee and conversation. The bartender had closed down the bar, but remained at his station, offering soda and water to anyone who asked. Mom had been solicited for two further events. I'd witnessed the exchange between her and the interested parties and the brochure with an attached business card she'd slipped into their hands.

I bent my elbow, pivoting my wrist to check the time on my watch. I stifled a yawn.

"Past your bedtime?"

I jerked around, forgetting my determination to move slowly around Arlo. I couldn't help it. He'd startled me. "Yes," I said, "yes, it is."

He smiled; a slow and lazy gesture that could have been from exhaustion. Whatever the cause, I liked how it looked, how it made me feel. I noted the camera bag slung from his shoulder and glanced around for the larger containers in which he transported the lights and

reflectors he'd used earlier.

"All ready to go?" I asked.

"I put everything else in the Jeep a little while ago, so, yes." He stood with his feet slightly apart, an infinitesimal swaying to his body. I detected a tensing in him, muscles tightening as he regained control over his balance. He slid his finger beneath the strap to his bag, pulling the slipping case back up.

"I'll walk out with you," I said.

His lips curved again.

The temperature had dropped considerably. I hugged myself as we crossed the lot to the family side, to Arlo's dusty Jeep parked in the glow thrown by one of the many old-fashioned lantern-style lights illuminating the parking spaces from their poles. Nearing his vehicle, I saw something move inside. When we got within a couple feet the driver's side door opened. A woman stepped out bundled in a winter coat, a scarf and earmuffs. I wondered if she'd been waiting long. I wondered who she was. Not someone from the party. She wore jeans and boots, not fancy dress.

"All set, Arlo?" She turned her gaze to me. "Hi."

"Hi," I said, step slowing.

She held out her hand. "I'm Jenny."

"Susan," I said, shaking it. "Suze." I let go, my hand slapping down to my side.

With an ease from casual and frequent association, she flipped open the back to Arlo's Jeep. He lowered the camera bag inside, Jenny patted his arm, shut the hatch. He turned to face me.

"Well," he said.

"Well," I echoed and added, a few beats too late and confused by my hesitation, "have a good night. I…I look forward to seeing the photos." Dumb thing to say. Why would I be seeing them?

"Okay," he said. I breathed in, released the air, lungs deflating. Arlo turned and got into the Jeep's passenger side. With a wave, Jenny climbed behind the wheel. I backed away to give her room to pull the vehicle out. The brake lights shone red on the gravel, my shoes. Arlo's hand lifted in my direction behind the glass before he turned to say something to Jenny, this Jenny person no one had bothered to mention to me.

I went back inside the barn to finish up the night.

Chapter Six

Mom shoved a mug filled with hot cocoa across the table in my direction. It slopped a little up the sides, rocking the floating marshmallow. I pulled the mug closer, inserting my nose over the steam. "I really just wanted to go to bed," I said.

"Really?" she responded, as if shocked. Maybe the shock truly existed. Maybe she thought her daughter took after her in more ways than looks. Maybe she thought the entire world was made from sterner stuff, the same stuff that appeared to be her composition. Because yes, after a long, activity-filled day, my mother did emerge as energized and fully awake. I heaved a sigh that rolled the cocoa steam into a great, big curve. Mom sat down across from me with her own mug.

"So," I said, "what's up?" Besides you, I thought. Dad had gone to bed sometime between my retrieving the corkscrew and Mom and I stumbling in the door with arms full of things she didn't want to leave out in the barn.

"What do you mean?" She took a careful sip from the steaming liquid.

"I figure you wanted to talk or something," I mumbled, frowning down at the marshmallow slowly melting.

"About what?"

I made a noise like my lovely old Scottish neighbor, deep in my throat. "I don't know. Pick a topic. Otherwise, I'm going to fall asleep in my

chocolate."

"Are you dating anyone?"

My eyebrows arched. "Excuse me?"

"I'm picking a topic."

"Don't bother with that one. It's a one-word answer: no. Next?"

"How's work?"

I sighed again, lifted my mug, tried to confiscate the marshmallow with my tongue. No luck. "It's…work," I said. "Nothing new going on. But it's more than my job, Mom, it's my business."

"I know. I'm glad you were able to reschedule everyone so you could come home."

"Me, too." I meant it. Goodness, how I meant it, despite all my inner griping. I'd never been fool enough not to recognize the value of a place, a person, a thing merely because it had the capability to annoy me. I could be plenty annoying myself and I knew some people valued me.

"Okay, then, let's talk about Christmas," Mom said.

"Christmas. All right. What's the plan of attack?"

"The what?" Her brow wrinkled.

"I don't mean it that way. I mean, how are we going to get everything accomplished in the next few days? I'm sure you have a long list you would already have been checking off if it hadn't been for the wedding."

Her shoulders dropped, her right hand coming up to rub at her eyes. She finally looked as though her energy had begun to flag. "You're right," she said.

"Can I see it?"

"See what?"

"The list, Mom. I know you have a physical list lurking around here somewhere. Let's have it."

"In the morning." She sipped at her cocoa, clutching the warm mug close to her face after. "We'll tackle it over breakfast, make our battle plan." Her lips curved. "There's something I need to tell you. I'm supposed to be keeping it a secret, but it's added a great deal to what there is to do."

"Okay," I drawled, "spill."

She sat back, closed her eyes, a drawn-out grin spreading across her face. "Shepherd's coming home, Suze, with Malory and her parents, and her younger sister. A much younger sister? I think she's fourteen

or fifteen."

I let out a whoop, quickly stifled so as not to wake Dad. "I can't believe it. All of us home for the holidays this year. I—wait. Is everyone staying in your house?"

"Yep," Mom said.

"Oh, crud," I said, "you'd better break out that list now."

She did not, but we discussed briefly some items on it while we finished our hot cocoa. She freely admitted certain bedrooms hadn't seen a vacuum or a dust rag in more months than she cared to count.

"My house isn't half as big as yours nor am I half as busy, but the entirety of my place is probably in the same condition." I brought our mugs to the sink and
washed them both, turning them upside down to drain and dry in the rack. "We'll get them spruced up, Mom, don't you worry."

"I'm not worried," she said.

"Good." I started toward the hallway, pausing with my hand on the switch to the light above the kitchen table. Mom pushed back her chair and stood,

following me up the stairs. Outside the room where I'd been sleeping, she gave me a quick, warm embrace. "Sleep well," I whispered into her fragrant hair.

"You, too."

I watched her walk down the hallway. As she closed the bedroom door, hers and Dad's, I called out: "Who's Jenny?" but not loudly, not loud enough for her to hear me or to answer. I don't think I wanted to know.

*　*　*

In the morning, Mom and I made a new list. We made it from hers, but divvied up projects between us on separate paper. I stuck mine in my pocket along with a pencil and she did the same.

"Shepherd's coming home," I said, grinning at her. "And we'll finally meet Malory in person. The phone, even FaceTime, doesn't quite cut it."

We'd all been sent photos and videos from their wedding, but like the phone, it wasn't the same as physically spending time with my new sister-in-law, or my older brother for that matter. I knew Mom

felt the same.

We went our separate ways, furniture polish and rags in hand. I cleaned the other three bedrooms, including changing out the sheets that had been languishing on the unused beds for who knew how long. Mom tackled downstairs. I washed the windows—something I rarely bothered with at my house unless I caught sight of some obvious smear in the sunlight—and vacuumed the curtains when I brought the vacuum up to do the floors. Confiscating three leftover poinsettias from Carla's wedding, I placed one to a dresser, hung a wreath on each mirror and lined the windows with strands of warm-white Christmas lights. Afterward, I stood back with my fists on my hips, the dust rag hanging from one, and felt extraordinary pleased with my efforts.

I checked my watch. Record time. I went to see how far Mom had gotten.

Finding her still in the living room, I whipped out my list and crossed off everything from the bedrooms with a flourish. "Ha! How far are you?"

"It's not a race, Suze." She sounded oddly subdued, perhaps a little dazed. I rushed to her side.

"Mom? Are you okay?"

"I just got off the phone—"

I grabbed her arm, thinking it could only be bad news. "Sit down."

"I…I don't need to sit down," she said. "I need a new list."

"Why?"

"Maybe I will sit down." She plopped her rump onto a sofa cushion, hands folded together between her knees. "I might have…I think…well, I did mention to some of the family, some that weren't involved in the secret, about Shepherd and Malory coming."

"Uh-oh," I said. It slipped out the way words sometimes do when you're not intending to say them. I sat down too, right next to her.

"Your dad's sister called, said they'd all been talking. I'm not sure who the heck 'all' are, but you know your Aunt Charlotte, it could be the world. She said to expect some calls, because they thought, since no one was at the wedding, how wonderful it would be if everyone converged on my house on Christmas Eve."

"She didn't use those exact words, did she?"

"No. But close enough. So I had to quick call Shepherd, right in the middle of his work day, to see what he thought of it. He'd apparently received a few calls himself and was going to talk to me once he got home this evening." She bit her lip, blew a breath out her nose. "There's not enough room in here," she muttered.

"Hello, Mom," I circled my fingers around her wrist, testing her pulse to see if it matched the panic on her face. "You have a whole venue right there in the barn that just housed well over a hundred people. We can manage an impromptu family reunion, don't you think? This is what you do."

She eyed me askance, flicked her gaze to the empty hallway, then up at the small, antique clock on the narrow fireplace mantel. "Don't they have anything better to do at Christmas?"

"Mom," I whispered, "this is the best thing to do at Christmas."

She released another breath, a long, slow one, and clapped her hands on her thighs, inadvertently shaking mine off. She stood, suddenly animated.

"Okay, let's finish cleaning down here, make some calls. We need numbers, a real headcount. Then we can plan a menu, including what certain people could bring with them. I'll still bake cookies, can't skip that. Carla didn't want any of the décor she paid for, so we can reuse what her guests didn't take with them. I'll hold onto the table linens that weren't soiled and send them all back after Christmas We should have music, Christmas music. I have a boatload of holiday cds and that old player of yours."

She went on for another several minutes before she wound down, turning mid-pace to look at me. I still hadn't gotten up, using my list's blank side to scribble down all she was saying.

"What are you doing?"

"Taking notes," I answered, pencil poised.

"Good idea." She walked from the room. A moment later I heard her rattling around in the kitchen. I followed.

"What's up, Mom?"

"Making a fresh pot of coffee," she said. "I don't think I'm going to get through the day without more."

"Why are you stressing out? How many hundreds of times have you done this?"

She glanced at me, the coffee pot in her hand filling with cold water beneath the running spigot. "This is different. This is family."

"Yes, this is family," I said. "Family is better, isn't it? What do you think they're going to expect on such short notice? A wedding reception to make up for the fact none of us got to go?"

Her eyes glazed over in contemplation. The water started bubbling from the pot into the sink. I hurried to her side, took it away and shut the spigot off. "Mom, stop. Stop, stop, stop. Go sit. I'll make the coffee."

She didn't move. I danced around her, gathering what I needed, filled the machine, turned it on. Leaning against the counter, I studied her face. "It'll be fun. It doesn't have to be the posh party of the season. Remember who we're talking about here."

"Right." Mom retrieved last night's mugs from the drain board. "None of us made it to your wedding either," she said, not quite out of the blue considering the conversation. My heart performed a funny thump, though.

"That was a long time ago, and I didn't have one, you know that. We got married and afterward had dinner with a couple of friends. Nothing else. Good thing. What a colossal money-waster it would have been for a marriage that didn't last out the year."

"Do you think you'll ever get married again?"

I stared at her, considered not answering. Pulling out the coffee pot, I stuck a mug underneath the flow to catch it and poured from the pot into Mom's cup, after which I performed a handy reversal with mine and waited for the coffee to finish, arms crossed.

"Suze?"

"Marriage isn't every girl's dream," I said.

Her lips scrunched up. She didn't speak.

"As I told Carla yesterday, it would probably be worthwhile to find someone I love and who loves me in return first. Don't you think?"

"Yes," she said. "Yes, I do."

"Great. Let's divvy up this new list then, shall we? Do any of these folks text? It would be a lot easier and more efficient than spending the rest of the day on the phone."

We agreed on texting. All talk of my erstwhile

marriage ceased. To be honest, I'd given my brief married life very little thought over the past near-decade. We'd both been ridiculously young. Not that age always mattered, but in my case and his, it clearly had.

Texting, receiving initial responses, writing down the definite affirmatives and the volunteered foodstuffs took up the remaining morning hours and a quarter of the afternoon, especially as some relatives decided it would be simpler to call back rather than type in their answers. Both my fingers and my voice had grown a little weary with the task. I hadn't talked to this many family members since Simon and Lucy got married.

At one point I snuck off to the kitchen to dip a tablespoon into the peanut butter jar. We'd agreed not to pause for lunch until all contact had been made, but I was starving. Mom came in right as I stuck the spoon in my mouth. Wordlessly, I reached behind me into the drawer for another and held it and the open jar out to her. She dug in, twisting the spoon for a hefty scoop.

"What about Arlo?"

I frowned at her question, the spoon glued to my tongue and my thoughts jumping from place to place, speculating on her meaning.

"Should we get him for photos?"

Oh. "Everyone has phones," I managed around the stickiness.

She shot me an odd look, stuck her spoon in her mouth. I turned away to rinse my utensil, drop it into the dishwasher, ignore her weighty gaze on my back.

"I just thought—"

I pivoted on my heel. "It's not worth the unexpected expense though, is it? We'll all be taking pictures. We can share them."

"Okay," she said, "that's smart." But she didn't sound convinced. Her gaze remained on my person as though I had suddenly announced I'd be running off with the postman. Befuddled, maybe disappointed. I waited for her to say something else. When she didn't, I retrieved the scribbled list from the counter, glanced down.

"What next?"

And so it went, on through the day, Mom and I whittling down the itemized chores, her occasional mentioning of Arlo's name in conjunction

with other topics, not quite obvious, but obvious enough. She'd recognized my interest, I knew. This led me to the conclusion she didn't know about Jenny, marching me to the further conclusion I wouldn't be able to get any information about the woman from her, even if I wanted to—which I didn't. Blatant curiosity could never be an excuse for mining into a near-stranger's life. This is what I told myself.

Eventually she gave up and moved onto other spaces in the house. Relieved, I drifted into a silent cleaning pattern. I ended up out on the back porch sweeping debris from the centerpieces off the tables and into a dustpan with a rag. Most of those had gone home with guests after the reception, and no wonder: they were beautiful.

A low flying red-tail hawk caught my eye out the window. I went closer to the glass, watched it sweep gracefully over the fields, hunting for rodents, I supposed, or merely enjoying the wind supporting its wings. I wanted to feel a bit more like that sometimes, ignoring the hunt for the necessities in life for the enjoyment of living it. Everyone probably

experienced that longing, now and again. And I had a job, a practice, and was, as Mom had pointed out, good at it. Lately though I missed what I could only term my roots. I missed this place, I missed the way it felt, I missed my family and the friends I'd left behind. Yes, I spoke with my family fairly regularly, and the friends to catch up on occasion, but it wasn't the same.

If I came back here, though, what would I do? Therein lay the dilemma. Giving up a successful endeavor for uncertainty seemed a ridiculously idiotic thing to do. Too risky, for one. Too irresponsible. Too self-indulgent. Too much like I was giving up.

I opened the back door and stepped outside, the chill air striking my bare face and hands in a tiny slap. I headed toward the greenhouse with no particular objective. With long strides, not a slow meander, I reached the glass structure in no time. I peered through the windows to make certain I wouldn't disturb any tender plants by opening the door, and then slipped inside. It smelled like soil and moisture in there. Like mint, too, and lavender, making me look more closely at the rows of planting

boxes. At the very back two boxes were green with wild spearmint, transplanted presumably from outside. Gardening gloves lay to one side and a small pair of child's scissors.

I touched a leaf, rubbed it between thumb and forefinger, brought my hand to my nose and sniffed. A smile crept onto my face, the scent comforting and familiar. Above the mint several wooden dowels hung suspended from the ceiling. From them, lavender tied with twine into bunches had been left to dry.

I had no idea what Mom intended to do with these herbals, but here, as everywhere, I found evidence of her industrious, constantly planning nature. If only I had a plan, a single plan, I might figure out what to do.

The door opened behind me. I whipped around. Mom stepped inside, latching the door against the breeze.

"I saw you from the sewing room," she said.

"You're not actually cleaning the sewing room? No one's going to go in there."

"I know they're not. That's why I figured it would be a good place to hide some things I have no

idea what to do with.”

“Good thinking.” I sniffed my mint-scented fingers again. “Love that spearmint.”

“It makes tasty mint jelly. Tea, too. You’ll have to have some.”

“Okay,” I said, suddenly awkward, suddenly blinking back tears.

Mom eased past me, reaching up to check the lavender’s condition. Several dried bits fell onto her hand. She held them out to me, fingers spread, the tiny purple flowers cupped in her palm. “Smell that.”

“Oh my goodness,” I cried after a deep breath, “that’s wonderful.”

“Isn’t it?” She set the petite petals aside on the wood ledge reluctant, no doubt, to toss them away. Lifting her head, she continued studying the drying lavender. Her signature ponytail had come loose as always, the band tying it back having slipped a good three inches from her nape, liberated strands rioting about her face and neck.

“Are you ever going to tell me what’s wrong?” she asked without looking at me.

“Of course I am,” I whispered.

"Now seems like a good time."

"Does it? I…I'm too old to be so…unable to move forward."

"How old are you?" she asked, facing me.

"What, you don't remember?"

"Of course I do. I just want you to say it out loud."

I backed up against a potting box, planting my hips against it, arms crossed. "I'm thirty-three."

"Not old," Mom said. "Not by a long shot."

"Yeah, well, too old to be so undecided, too old to be crying my woes to my mother."

"Needing someone to talk to, someone who has known you your entire life, loved you your entire life, isn't something you outgrow. You don't think I miss my mom still for that very reason?"

I started crying in earnest, head-in-my-hands spearmint-scent-and-all type weeping. To her credit, Mom didn't rush to take me into her arms. She stood very still and quiet, her hands together in front of her, waiting. Giving me time, time to finish bawling, time to recall the strength I actually did possess, the strength I'd learned from her. I finally stopped, wiping the tears away with my sweatshirt sleeve. I

looked at her through my filmy vision, sniffling.

"Let's go have some of that spearmint tea right now," she said, "shall we?"

In silent, grateful agreement, I followed her back inside.

Chapter Seven

Only three days until Christmas Eve, so only two more days to accomplish everything on Mom's constantly appended list. The nervous breakdown I'd thought she'd been heading for right after her phone call from Aunt Charlotte had clearly been avoided and forgotten. Dad remained his usual go-with-the-flow self. Simon had arrived with the kids and Lucy to lend

a hand later Sunday afternoon, after my talk with Mom. A talk we hadn't discussed since. I remembered it though, nearly word for word. It hadn't been a long conversation. More time had been spent in consuming tea than in speech. The silences, the many silences, had contained no unspoken judgment, no undue concern.

"Whatever you decide," Mom had said at the end of it, removing our teacups from the table, "you know your dad and I are there for you."

I hadn't briefly spilled my soul because I wanted them to feel responsible in any manner, and I understood from Mom's face she didn't. Her sentiment had been uttered in the very literal, comforting sense.

Now, standing in the Monday morning sunshine on the sidewalk in Connor Falls proper, I pulled the most recent list from my jacket pocket and went over the baked goods bordered with a penciled box. Some folks were bringing their best holiday confections, but not enough for all who were attending. Simon still insisted he'd bake bread, but Mom, fearful he might throw up his hands in defeat if the loaves didn't turn out as planned, wanted to arrange for fresh-baked rolls and several extra pies. I hurried into From the Hart Bakery and gave my order to the young girl behind the counter. Gina was nowhere in sight, leaving me unable to

exchange a quick hello. I would have liked to see her before I left. I wasn't sure if that would happen now.

Next, my Christmas gift for Simon, which had also expanded to gifts for Malory's sister, her parents, and I supposed Shepherd and Malory themselves, since I couldn't be sure their package from me would arrive before they flew out to come home. I decided to make it simple and headed to Sophie's Chandlery again. She had lotions and soaps so something like that would work for the sister, since I knew nothing about her. I'd make sure the scent wasn't too strong. Two cheery, holiday-scented candles would be nice for Shepherd and Malory as well as for the in-laws, and not a problem for the return flight. My brother and his new wife would have the journals waiting for them when they got home.

After exiting the candle shop, I headed again to the bookstore. Simon did so enjoy baking, although two years after the bug had bitten him, he remained in the learning stages. There had to be a book with exciting but not overwhelming recipes for bread-making. I didn't want to frustrate him, after all.

I approached the same young man who'd helped me the other day and asked him to point me in the right direction. Setting my package down by my feet, I

started pulling out books to examine. A voice carried to me from the next aisle over. Open book in hand, I paused, listening despite myself.

"I don't know what you're so upset about," said a woman's voice.

"I'm not upset, only concerned."

I recognized the male voice. Arlo.

Now I was in a quandary. I had business in this section and didn't want to walk away until I'd concluded my search, but I didn't want to eavesdrop either. Making my way around the corner, saying a quick hello and returning to look for Simon's book might be the best course. Arlo would be warned away from saying something personal and I wouldn't look like an imbecile if he caught me within earshot, having said it. Clutching the promising book I hadn't fully perused and picking up my bag, I stepped around the shelving.

"Hi," I said, "I thought that was you."

Oh.

Well.

Jenny.

"I'm sorry, I didn't mean to interrupt." I started to turn away.

"Susan," Arlo said. "Don't go."

Against my better judgment, I didn't. I waited. "Shopping?" he asked.

I gave the bag a shake. "Yes, last-minute gifts. My older brother and his wife and family are coming. It was supposed to be a surprise." I shrugged my shoulder in a slow lift. "Also, there's an impromptu and huge family gathering now on Christmas Eve."

He smiled, glanced at Jenny and back at me. His eye contact lasted longer than usual. I wondered if my practiced, relative immobility could be paying off.

"Might be a good idea if you didn't have extra mouths to feed on Christmas Day, then?" he said. "S— seems like you all have enough going on."

"Oh, no!" I was, perhaps, somewhat more emphatic than I should have been. Beside him, Jenny's eyes widened. "Don't be silly." I continued. "You don't want to disappoint Mom when she's putting a spread on."

"I'd never want to disappoint your mother," he said. He meant it, I could tell.

"Arlo," Jenny said, her hand on his arm, "you don't have to say yes to an invitation just because someone feels sorry for you."

My breath huffed out in shock at the nerve of her. I couldn't let the statement go undefended.

"My Mom doesn't feel sorry for Arlo. No one in my family does, as a matter of fact. My mother invited him because she views him as a friend." I slapped the cookbook up against my chest, clutched the Chandlery bag handle tight. "We will see you Christmas day?" I didn't wait for an answer, from either of them. "Good." I strode to the counter, paid for the cookbook and departed without looking back.

Still grumbling inwardly from the encounter when I arrived at Hummingbird Farm, I stomped up the porch steps and into the house, continuing straight up the stairs to deposit the two bags on my bed. I stood for several minutes without removing my coat, staring out through the window glass to the blue sky.

Was that what he thought? Was that what Arlo really thought? That we felt *sorry* for him? Or might this be only Jenny's perception? Nothing could be further from the truth. My mom especially never bothered with something as detrimental as feeling sorry for a person. Feeling sorry for someone didn't do anyone any good. Caring helped. Recognizing a person's strengths and encouraging them helped. Taking time to listen helped. Pity did nothing except make the recipient feel worse, as if their condition held some shameful connotation.

Growling, I unclenched my fists, yanked off my gloves. I tossed them on the bedspread next to the bags, followed by my coat. Remembering the list in the pocket, I snatched it out, checking to make sure I hadn't forgotten anything in my outrage. Nope, all good.

Mom called me from below. "Coming, Mom," I answered in my best Emma Watson imitation. Mom wouldn't recognize it. I didn't think she'd seen any Harry Potter movies, at least not more than once. I went downstairs. As soon as she spotted my compliance, she returned to the kitchen, slipping the damp dishtowel in her hand over the oven door handle. She smoothed the fabric out.

"Everything go well in town?" she asked, brushing back her flyaway strands.

"Hunky-dory," I said. "This list can go in the trash. How about here? No calls?"

"One."

I kept silent, anticipating Arlo's name along with a cancellation for Christmas dinner.

"Alice. She's bringing a whole turkey with stuffing. Fully cooked, since she hasn't far to come."

Having expected nothing resembling Mom's words, I found myself momentarily lacking in response. "Oh—oh good," I finally stammered. "Did you get a

chance to add it to the chart?" I headed that way in case she hadn't, to the chart on copy paper hanging on the refrigerator door. Baker's twine attached to the magnet holding it in place held a pen at its nether end. I snatched the pen up, clicked out the point. "Ah, you did already."

"As soon as I hung up the phone," Mom said.

I nodded, lips twisting. No surprise there. Straightening, I released the pen, letting it swing. I felt tempted to bring up my conversation with Arlo and his girlfriend in the bookstore, but Mom was the last person I wanted to be troubled by an insensitive remark. She was used to them occasionally coming from me, unfortunately, but Jenny had made a rash judgment without proof or merit. I calmed myself before Mom picked up on the annoyance in my body language. She'd always been way too good at reading people.

"So what time are Shepherd and the rest getting in again?" I asked, for something to say. I knew their flight landed three-thirty-ish.

She repeated the information. Simon was lending me the only vehicle among us that could accommodate four extra adults and a teenager together with their luggage. ABE wasn't that far away. I could handle a

minivan for the short trip. Even so, I made Simon promise to bring it over early, telling him I was paranoid about not leaving enough time. Truthfully, I wanted to practice driving it up and down the driveway. I hadn't owned a car bigger than a compact since day one.

He would have laughed at me, had he known. He probably would also have insisted he pick them up himself rather than letting me drive his van, but he had work and I didn't, so I had no plan to reveal my anxiety until after my return from the airport.

"Ready to make some candy?" Mom interjected into my overlong silence.

"Candy?" I echoed. "What happened to cookies? Cookies are on list number three."

"I've scratched them off for this year," Mom said, tapping the list taped to the cabinet door. "Seems like everyone is making a favorite to bring. So, I thought I'd make candy instead. I bought boxes over the summer when I first had the idea. We'll fill each one with candy and wrap them up with ribbon."

"Huh."

"What?"

"I have an idea, Mom. Why don't we skip the candy, too?"

She jerked her head back, affronted. "Why?"

"Because…because there's enough to do. We have enough sweets to rot everyone's teeth from their heads. If you don't kill yourself with all of this, you're going to kill your one and only daughter. And because you and I are going to take a breather and go to lunch." I checked my watch. "Brunch. No arguments."

She stared at me in silence. To give her credit, the silence and the stare lasted no more than two seconds. She sighed.

"Okay, let me get my coat."

"You might want to brush your hair while you're at it," I called after her. I understood now where I got the blasé attitude about simple daily habits. It struck me like an epiphany, one that made me laugh and reach up to check I hadn't gone through the morning's shopping sporting bedhead. Especially, you know, in front of Jenny.

With a noise resembling a cross between a frantic bird and a distressed puppy, I rushed up the stairs to find my comb.

*   *   *

"This is very nice of you, taking your old Ma to

brunch," my old ma said from across the table. "I can't remember the last time I've been out to eat during the day."

"Frankly, I can't either. I used to go out to lunch every now and then, but I've taken to eating in the office." I opened my menu. We'd decided on Shelly's, a family-friendly place known for its reasonably priced diner style offerings. Any evening you'd likely find families filling nearly every table. On a weekday just before noon, however, my mom and I were two of only a dozen or so patrons in the place. Like the other establishments in Connor Falls, the restaurant had been decorated for the holidays. Shelly's relied on the vintage for its special appeal. The decorations reminded Mom of her childhood. She had something to say about almost every one. I had to stop her by opening her menu, too, and sliding it across to her.

"Oh," she exclaimed, distracted but excited anew, "they have actual brunch specials."

I rolled my eyes and turned my attention to the selections. They had quaint names. Mom pointed out that the names had been taken from song lyrics from the nineteen-sixties and seventies.

"Cute," I said. She picked up on my tone right away, unintentional though it had been.

"Grumpy, are we?"

"No. I said 'cute', didn't I? I just don't remember some of these lyrics, I guess. Oh, this one, and this one, too. You still play this music sometimes."

"All the time," she said. "You're not around to hear it. And don't take offense. That's a statement of fact, not a criticism."

"Gotcha." I lifted my menu closer, ducked my head.

"I miss you, Suze."

The menu dropped, splat, on the table. "I miss you, too, Mom. You know I do."

"I do. What are you having?"

Glad for the changing subject, I decided on the *Back to the Garden*, a scrumptious-sounding salad with spinach and fruit both dried and fresh and candied pecans for good measure. The menu promised the salad was small, since it also came with a slice of quiche. Mom decided to have the same right as the server approached, pad in hand. We both sat back, awkwardly smiling at each other as she left with our orders.

"So how long are you giving yourself?" Mom asked, harkening back to our conversation the day before. I'd assumed she'd have more questions.

I turned my head to the window, to a woman with

a child passing by on the sidewalk. "I'd say as long as it takes, but that's really too open-ended and I might never decide."

"Yep," she said, "you're probably right. That's why I mark things on the calendar, the physical calendar. Simon gets on me about it, telling me to set reminders on my phone, put things on the pretend calendar, because that's why those apps or whatever they're called are there. I say baloney sauce. The real calendar is what works for me."

I looked back at her. "I'm pretty sure they're both real calendars," I said, taking a swallow from my water glass. "But I get it. Believe me, I do."

"I see the calendar every day, multiple times a day. It's a much more efficient reminder for me. Plus, I love the picture reveal every month. This year, it's national parks. Beautiful."

"Don't let Simon try to tell you what to do. You're you. You're independent and have your own way of doing things that works for you just fine. His way is great for him. That doesn't mean it's great for everybody else in the world and even if it was, so what? You do what you do, period."

She smiled, lips closely curling. "You're so much like me."

"I know. I know I am. You're lucky you have Dad. He's happy with who you are. Any man who thinks they're attracted to me hightails it out of there when they get a whiff of how little I really need a man around the house…so to speak. They're good for some things." I rolled my eyes again. Mom guffawed, almost losing the tea she'd sipped. She covered her mouth with her hand.

"Oh, honey," she said, "you have such a way with words."

"I try."

Our meals arrived. Temporarily talked out and both hungry, we ate without intermission for a good ten minutes. The fruit combo in the salad was particularly tasty. I committed the contents to memory so I could make it myself sometime.

"Who's that?" Mom said, lowering her fork to her plate. I turned my head, following her gaze. On the corner, waiting to cross the street, stood Arlo and Jenny. Arlo looked tired, as if he'd had enough for one day. Jenny was chattering away like a bird.

"That's Jenny," I said.

"Who?"

"Jenny. I don't know her last name. She and Arlo are together apparently."

I went back to my salad, to remembering everything in it. I felt Mom's eyes on me.

"When did you meet her?" she asked. Her nonchalant tone didn't fool me. She might even have been a little miffed at not having known before. She and Arlo did seem close. I was surprised he hadn't mentioned Jenny to her.

"She was waiting in his Jeep for him Saturday night after the wedding reception. To drive him home. I do remember him mentioning he doesn't drive at night right now. And then…and then I ran into them both in the bookstore earlier."

I refused to tell Mom what she'd said. I absolutely would not.

Mom set the napkin from her lap onto the table. "I'll get the scoop. Shall I?" She started to get up. I reached over the table and grabbed her hand.

"Mom, no. Please don't. You can interrogate him next time you see him, okay?"

She settled back down. I released her hand. She spread her napkin on her lap again, picked up her fork. "But you like him," she said.

I dipped my head a little to the side, spearing a strawberry. "I don't know him, so..."

Mom let out a long, slow, quiet breath before

digging into her quiche. I appreciated her keeping any further questions to herself, because I really didn't know how I'd answer them.

Later that night, when the house was once again quiet, Mom and Dad tucked up in their bed, I went for another midnight walk. This time I bundled up more warmly so I could stay out longer. I snuck out from the back porch and headed straight into the fields. My breath frosted, the stars shone, my boots cracked the thoroughly frozen vegetation. With my hat tucked down around my ears, I only heard my footsteps on last season's corn stalks in muffled repetition.

I had decisions to make, decisions that could never include Arlo, no matter how much I'd like to get to know him if not for Jenny. They couldn't include my family either, not really. These decisions had to be solely about me, so they'd be clear, definite, well-reasoned. And so I'd have no one to blame if they didn't work out, I added with a snort in the dark.

Christmas was coming, days away. The family, a great many members, would all be together for the holiday. It would be nice if I could reach a resolution by then, come to terms with it, perhaps share my plans with others, move forward. My heart-brain wanted one thing, while my logical-brain insisted on pointing out

all the arguments against. It liked to do so with particular emphasis during the night, when things like sleep yearned contrarily for the upper hand.

"Ah, who needs sleep," I muttered out loud as I trudged my way further afield. Again, I spotted deer at a distance, only two, observing me with caution. Some lone traveler scuttled away low to the ground. I heard a car on the road, a rumbling hum, coming toward Hummingbird Farm, passing it, disappearing over the crest. I paused and turned around, looking back at the house. Starlight reflected in a pale gleam off the windows that weren't lit by the clear twinkle lights. This close to Christmas Mom and Dad kept them on through the night.

Realizing I wouldn't likely come to any decisions bleary-eyed and tripping over the terrain in the darkness, I debated going back…for about thirty seconds. Instead, I tugged my hat down lower, shoved my hands in my pockets, and walked on. Before long, I found myself approaching the bordering woodland. The closely grown brush at its edge looked impassable without a machete and the shadows beyond stretched black indeed. An owl hooted nearby, very nearby. I tipped my head back and looked around, spotting its shape, its eyes glowing in the dark. I'd read somewhere

that owls didn't possess eyeballs per se, but that their eyes were shaped like tubes and held in place in bone, which was why they turned their heads in all directions to see with their wonderful binocular vision. I kept myself still so as not to frighten it away. After a moment, the bird launched itself from the branch where it had been sitting and sailed off into the forest in absolute silence.

I released my breath, trying to follow the owl's path with my own comparatively ineffectual eyesight. I lost it within no more than twenty feet, but my gaze landed on something else. Not quite sure what I looked at, I moved to the side, trying to find a way into the trees. Neither Mom nor Dad had ever mentioned another building on their property. I glanced back, making sure I hadn't left their acreage. I appeared not to have done, at least relative to the boundary lines they'd pointed out in the past.

Breaking out my phone, I turned on the flashlight and held it high above my head in order to prevent the tangled shadow from nearby branches blocking my view. I glimpsed fieldstone walls and empty window casements and a slate roof which looked, in spite of the weathering, to be in halfway decent shape. At least it wasn't falling in. No more than a storey tall, I figured

the structure might be a long-forgotten outbuilding. After all this time, anything might be living beneath that roof. Once again, I stood in debate about returning to Mom and Dad's, this time because the unknown building seemed to be drawing me in. I genuinely wanted to see it, its exact shape and size, whether it had become a decrepit wreck or was a well-built aging edifice doing its level best to withstand the elements and the passing years, whether or not it could be salvaged, repaired, renovated, made livable for someone.

Made livable for someone like me.

In sudden, bursting clarity, I rushed back across the fields. I would need to see the building by day, of course, and there would be oh so many considerations, but in the instant I'd pictured myself living there, living back in Connor Falls, my heart-brain had burst out in joy and told my logical-brain to stuff it. I felt better than I had in many months.

Letting myself in the back door, I tiptoed up the stairs and into my room. I shirked from my coat and hat and gloves, kicked off my boots, threw myself down onto the bed with a pen and paper pad I'd snatched off the nightstand, ready to make notes, ready to make a list. My cheeks tingled in the room's warmth. I smelled

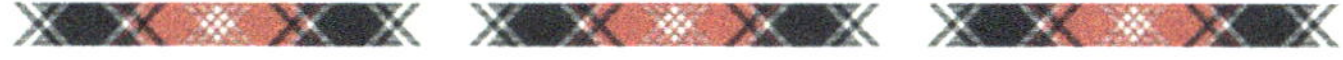

the frigid night air in my short, static-filled hair. I touched the pen's point to the ruled yellow paper, thinking, thinking hard about where to begin.

The next thing I knew morning had come, the sun burning bright once more upon my face. The pad lay beside me on the covers, five words printed and underscored at the top.

Susan Hardwick is coming home.

Chapter Eight

Dad, Mom and I hiked back across the fields before Simon's appointed time for dropping off his minivan. We brought loppers and a shovel, although why we might need the latter, I wasn't quite sure.

The forecast was calling for snow. I could smell it, see it in the pale gray cloud cover, hovering low. No one mentioned accumulation today beyond an inch or

two. Christmas Day might be another matter. I hoped the snow would hold off until I'd returned from pickup at the airport, though. Simon and Lucy's van did have front-wheel drive, but I'd gotten used to the all-wheel of my car when the weather took a turn. I kept reminding myself an inch or two was nothing. The cargo, however, was priceless and drivers on the road during the first snow could be somewhat nuts.

When we neared the place in the woods where I had located the building, I put airport shuttling from my mind.

"It's a lot of acreage," Mom was saying. "We haven't explored every inch of it. We haven't had any reason to."

"There's no accusation going on here, Mom. I just happened across it last night—"

"In the dark, alone," said my dad.

"In the dark, alone, yes. I'm just really curious. You can't tell me you both aren't, too. You wouldn't be traipsing out here with me right now if you weren't." I hadn't revealed to them the whole reason for my interest. Not yet. I still had things to work through, in my head and in my life.

Upon our approach, a fox darted from the underbrush, his rich red pelt brilliant in the wintery

illumination. Both my parents turned to watch the animal race across the stubbled field. I witnessed respect and awe in their eyes. My heart swelled. I couldn't help my admiration for them both. Once they pivoted to face me again, I pointed with the lopper handles. "Through there. I couldn't get in, but I could see it."

"Okay," said Dad, "let's get lopping."

While Mom stood leaning on the shovel, Dad and I pruned a path to the other side. Not a big one, only enough to pass through. We hadn't any reason for too much disturbance. I walked ahead of him toward the building looming in the still shadowed wood.

"Honey," he called back to my mother, "would you look at that?"

I heard them tramping in behind me, my mother giving a small cry like something had jabbed her, probably a barb from the multiflora rose growing everywhere. She came up next to me, sucking on her pinkie.

"You okay?" I asked.

"Fine."

Sweeping the lopper end back and forth across the groundcover, I went closer to the structure. In winter, snakes in Pennsylvania enter a state called brumation, a kind of partial dormancy. This building would be perfect habitat. I wanted to make sure not to disturb any. Dad appeared at my elbow with a large flashlight.

"Let's have a look, eh?"

The door stood wide, seemingly in decent shape, possibly because it opened inward and had been protected. Dad shone the light around. A wooden floor had suffered badly, boards missing here and there, but the entire building stood on a stone foundation, beneath which existed a cellar of some kind. The floor beams looked solid enough. Underneath, several feet down, I glimpsed a cobbled subterranean floor. All the building's windows were broken, some still retaining shards of ancient glass. The walls inside, what we could see, had no bow to them. Various timbered uprights remained solid. The flashlight didn't reveal insect damage or rot, but that could show up on closer examination. Flipping the beam up toward the roof, Dad swept the light from side to side. Several old barn swallow nests clung to the hand-hewn trusses. No daylight showed through underlayment or the slate above. My lips curved.

"It's beautiful," I said.

"Yeah, sort of," Mom agreed behind me. "I can see that."

"Be nice to resurrect it," said my dad.

"Yes," I answered him, "it would."

*   *   *

The snow held off. The first flakes didn't speckle the windshield until I pulled into the driveway with my passengers. None appeared worn out by their flight, chatting non-stop the whole ride. Malory's sister Nester possessed a heavy accent I couldn't understand half the time. I confessed myself charmed nevertheless. Mom and Dad must have been waiting at the window. They hurried out before I'd even put the van in park. Simon followed with Sammy and Stuart. He held his hand out for the keys from me the minute the introductions, hellos and hugs had concluded.

"Dad told me about you practicing in the driveway. If I'd known…"

"Oh for crying out loud," I said, dropping the keys onto his palm. "You're kidding, right?"

He swept around the vehicle, eyeing it for damage. Ignoring him, I set Sammy and Stuart to carrying smaller bags and I grabbed two others. The whole crowd of us piled on into Mom and Dad's, where more hasty greetings took place and then everyone was shown where they'd be sleeping by Mom. Dad took the two cases I'd been carrying. I went back outside.

"Did you see the front quarter panel?" I yelled to Simon. "I side-swiped an SUV when I exited the cell phone lot."

"Not funny," he said.

"I thought it was. If you were that worried, why didn't you go? You obviously had the time, since you're here."

"Honestly, I only finished up work about forty-five minutes ago. I wouldn't have been able to manage it."

I walked up to him and punched him in the upper arm. Lightly, I swear. "You're a dolt," I said.

Snowflakes fell with increasing volume, catching in my eyelashes, clinging to my hair, my coat sleeves. Slowing spinning, I lifted my face to them, eyes closed.

"What are you doing?" Simon asked.

"Reveling."

He snorted. We all had that habit, snorting. A fabulous tool was a snort, appropriately employed in so many exchanges, its meaning infinite. While I continued to spin, I heard the porch door open, rapid footsteps crossing the gravel. Someone snatched me from my feet, twirling me at a much faster rate than I'd been enjoying.

"Shepherd," I cried, opening my eyes, "put me down."

In appearance, Shepherd was a cross between our mom's father and Dad, but without Dad's height. When we were young, Simon and I used to insist he didn't look like anyone else and had been adopted. Hearing the taunt at one point, Mom broke out some photos of Granddad when he'd been a kid, effectively shutting us up. She'd also told us rather sternly that even if Shepherd had been adopted, he'd be as much family as if he'd been born to it. She hadn't been very happy with me and Simon that day. Funny how things came back to you. Family was family was family no matter what the configuration. Blood didn't matter. Love did.

I stepped back from Shepherd, my hands on his arms. I looked up into his face and Granddad's dancing eyes. "You've got a secret," I said.

"What? How do you know?"

"I can see it. Plain as day. You're bursting to tell."

"Okay, but you have to stay mum. You, too, Simon. For a bit anyway. Promise?"

Simon and I both nodded.

Shepherd leaned forward to whisper. "We're pregnant. Well, Malory is doing the actual carrying, but we're pregnant."

I threw my arms around his middle and hugged him, really, really hard. Simon slapped him on the

back.

"You do know the dress Malory's wearing isn't hiding that fact, don't you?" I said to Shepherd, whose grin nearly split his face. "I had my suspicions the minute she unbuttoned her coat to get in the van. You better tell Mom and Dad soon, because Mom's going to pick up on that, too."

The porch door opened again. A human squeal drew my eye around Shepherd in time to see Mom trotting down the steps toward us. Behind her, Malory shrugged palms up from the doorway. I poked Shepherd in the stomach with my forefinger.

"Secret's out, Shep," I said.

Following congratulations, we trooped inside, shaking snow from garments and shoes on the mat before entering. Voices and laughter bounced around the high ceilings, sounding as though twice as many people were housed beneath. Mom crooked her finger discreetly. I followed her into the kitchen.

She appeared downright giddy. "Great news, eh?" she said, turning to replenish the coffee pot with fresh stock. I couldn't help thinking how far away her new grandchild would be living, but I said nothing about that and agreed with enthusiasm.

"And what about your news?" she continued,

measuring hefty tablespoons of ground coffee into the filter. "Will you be sharing?"

"Not yet," I said. "That's okay, isn't it? It's not quite as fabulous as a new family member, after all."

She smiled, slapping the lid onto the coffee container. "It is to me."

I shook my head. "You're my mom. That's pretty much guaranteed."

"Ah, I wouldn't bank on that." She poured the water into the maker, turned it on and spun herself around to lean against the counter. She crossed her arms. "I possibly could have ended up not being able to stand your company. I got lucky though."

"Me, too."

We stood silently for a moment before she loosened her arms and reached back, tapping a knuckle on the nearest list hanging from the cabinet door by painters' tape. "I'm thinking we should hide these."

"Agreed," I said.

"And count them for now as done as they're going to get."

Again, I concurred, carefully peeling back tape from each paper and taking them down. We decided to tuck them away in the pantry temporarily, figuring no one would go digging there.

"And," she added, dragging out the word, "we'll spend the remainder of the evening hanging out with everyone. I say we order something in for dinner, too, because tomorrow's going to be another busy day."

One more time I assented. Arms looped together we headed into the living room, calling out for preferences. I had no idea what Malory's parents and sister would make of our casual dinner management, but we were one family now, take us or leave us.

* * *

The parents in bed, Lucy gone home with the boys, and Malory frankly asleep in the deep chair with the ottoman, Shepherd, Simon and I sat on the floor close to the flames leaping in the living room fireplace, the twinkling lights on the evergreen by the window the only other illumination in the room. Behind us, Nester lay curled on the sofa, an empty mug on the table nearby, the hot cocoa long gone from the interior. I'd glanced back twice expecting to find her asleep, but instead caught her watching us in silence, a small smile on her lips. I gathered we were amusing her somehow. It had been a long time since the three of us had been able to get together. We were harkening back to old tales and old times, no doubt bizarre and out of context to a sixteen-year-old who hadn't lived our collective past.

"So, got a man in your life?" Shepherd asked me unexpectedly.

"Oh my gawd," Nester said from the sofa. "Seriously, Shep? I wouldn't answer him if I were you," she added to me, swinging her legs off the cushions and sitting up. "Truly, I wouldn't bother. Him, he's got the idea everyone should be tucked up in a sweet little relationship." Despite her caustic words, the tone wasn't there and the smile she sent him fond. She went to her sister, shook her gently and pulled on her hands, urging her up from the chair. "Time for bed, sleepyhead."

Malory mumbled goodnight as they headed from the room to the stairs. Shepherd watched his wife disappear from sight with emotion raw on his face.

"I'm happy for you, Shep," I whispered.

"I'm happy for me too."

"You should be." I stood, gathering up Nester's mug and the two glasses on the hearth. "Anyone want something else?"

"You're avoiding my question," Shepherd said. "And yeah, I'll take another half glass of that mead, thanks. Simon?"

Simon lifted his hands. "I'm good. I'm heading

home soon."

Shepherd got up, followed me into the kitchen. He stood at my elbow as I deposited the mug and glasses into the sink and filled a fresh one with the locally brewed mead.

"Only half," he reminded me when I'd almost finished.

"Too late. You can break out a funnel, though, if you want to pour some back into the bottle."

Smirking, he reached into the cabinet for a tumbler and dumped a portion from his glass into the second one. He handed the tumbler to me.

"Thanks," I said, not really meaning it.

"Is there anyone in your life, sis? Come on, spill."

I experienced a quick leap in my head to Arlo—Arlo the man I barely knew, Arlo of the infamous Jenny/Arlo combination, Arlo with whom I'd hardly shared thirty minutes' conversation—and jumped away again. "Nope," I said. "Not a one."

"Is that why you're moving back home?"

I sputtered into the glass I held to my mouth, bubbling the honeyed contents. "Jeez, Shepherd!" I wiped my chin with my shirtsleeve. "Of course, that's not why. Who told you I was moving back anyway?"

"Dad. You are, aren't you? He said something

about a house out there in the woods they didn't even know existed."

I sighed, clunking the tumbler onto the counter. "He wasn't supposed to say anything."

"To be honest, Simon mentioned it first and then I asked Dad about the house and—"

"Simon knew?"

"Well, yeah."

I closed my eyes, exasperated with the whole blabbing lot. Maybe I should reconsider my plan. However, unless I kept every aspect in my life to myself for eternity these things would always get shared. Families didn't keep secrets. At least not the one I'd grown up in.

Opening my eyes again, I shot Shepherd a look before dumping the mead from the tumbler into the sink. I started rinsing all the dishes stacked in the basin. Shepherd yanked open the dishwasher for me so I could fit them inside.

"It's not a house," I said as I worked. "Not yet. It's more like an ancient, not very large outbuilding I'm hoping to restore and renovate. A number of trees will need to be cleared back from it. It'll need a well, septic, electric, a lane for access, permits…" I stopped, the enormity of my half-baked plan hitting me. I lifted my

gaze to the window, my face a ghostly reflection in the glass.

"Wow," said Shepherd quietly. "That's a project."

"Ain't it just?" I drawled.

"What made you decide to do this?"

"Roots."

"Like the PBS show?"

I huffed out a breath. "No. And that's called 'Finding Your Roots' by the way. I'm talking about my personal roots in the here and now. I've lived half a dozen places since moving away and not one ever felt quite like home to me. I still think of Connor Falls as home, whenever the word comes up. The place I live now? It's my house. That's how I hear it in my head. How I feel it. My house. Not my home. I want my home."

"You know, Suze, home is where the heart—"

"Don't say it. No, do say it, because my heart is here. Maybe if I had a significant other in my life, I might feel differently. But I don't think so. And I'm not going to base my decisions on that what-if anyway. I want to change my life. Part of that plan is coming home. I've been working through it for a while now. It was no quick decision, believe me. Seeing that building solidified my ideas somehow, yet even if I hadn't seen it, if I can't make the building work, I'll find someplace else here."

Shepherd shook his dark head. "Big changes in the offing, then."

"Big changes."

Simon came to find us, snuggling a folded blanket and a pillow against his chest. "Just texted Lucy. I'm crashing on the couch. See you at breakfast." He shuffled off back to the living room in his sock feet.

"I'm heading up, too," I said to Shepherd. "Enjoy your mead."

"Right behind you." He tossed off the remainder and deposited the glass in the dishwasher. We walked up the narrow stairs not quite side by side, parting ways in the hallway outside my door.

"I'd like to say I'll help you in whatever way you need," he said. "My arms may be long, but they're not quite long enough to reach across the ocean and wield a hammer. Still…"

"I know." I smiled at him. "You're going to have enough on your hands pretty soon anyway."

"Oh, yeah, right. I almost forgot about that."

"Baloney sauce," I said, using Mom's favorite

expression. He walked down the hall and paused at the open doorway to an even narrower staircase leading to the two attic rooms above.

"It must be nice to be so brave," he called softly along to me.

"Or stupid," I said. "We'll see."

Chapter Nine

Afraid I might oversleep, I picked up my phone to set an alarm for the morning—well, for later. It was already morning, the very wee hours of it. Christmas Eve. Someone had texted me from an unknown number.

Thanks for being understanding. Jenny can be overprotective sometimes. See you Christmas Day.

Enjoy your unexpected family reunion.

I sat down slowly on the mattress edge, clutching the phone in my hand. How had he gotten my number? Moreover, what was I supposed to do with his message? At an appropriate hour, I would respond in some vague way, but otherwise, I didn't quite know what to make of the text or why Arlo felt it necessary to send. I didn't need thanking. In fact, I thought my response to Jenny's statement hadn't been at all tactful or understanding. I'd been annoyed and figured I'd made that clear.

I slid the phone onto the nightstand, confused with how I felt about him contacting me at all. If not for Jenny, I would have been quietly thrilled. I did like him, despite barely knowing him. I supposed it happened like that sometimes, meeting new people and finding something in their company that pleased a part of you, made you want to know them better. But there was Jenny. No getting beyond that fact. His text hadn't implied anything other than a simple communication, and I was glad. I wouldn't have wanted him to be the guy who'd complicate or risk a relationship he already had.

Besides, with big changes coming, I didn't need a man in my life.

Yes, this was what I told myself as I shirked off my clothes and yanked on the tee shirt and sleep pants I wore for bed. I continued to tell myself the same thing while I shimmied under the covers, pulling them up to my chin. I said it aloud when I nearly jerked my arm from the socket in order to snatch up the phone and reread Arlo's message.

Nope, all innocence. No interest there. Good. Yep, good.

I snapped off the lamp and threw myself face down into my pillow.

Sunlight streamed into the room way too quickly. I knew upon greeting it, eyes wide, I had seriously overslept. Right through the alarm even. Or I'd turned it off without waking. Either way, I couldn't believe Mom hadn't come hunting for me with a vengeance.

Forgoing a shower for expediency, I hastily dressed and clomped down the stairs. I found only Mom and Dad in the kitchen. "Is everyone else still asleep?" I shot a glance to the clock, making sure I hadn't misread my phone.

"Nester is," Mom said, "but Shep took everyone else for a run into town to grab some pastries."

I reflected for a second on the whole order I'd recently placed.

"I know," Mom said, apparently reading my face. "I told them to pick those up, too. They may as well get what they want for breakfast, though. I'm sure after tonight there'll be nothing left of any of it."

"Maybe set some aside for Christmas Day?"

Mom grunted her agreement. Dad looked up from his coffee. "So, you ladies have lists, yes? Give me one and let's get this day going."

I laughed out loud and wrapped my arms around him in a huge hug. "Yes," I said, "and let's."

With Simon's help and Shepherd's when they returned, we five made short work of the final to-do's on our lists. Nester was quite helpful once she climbed from her bed, giving Mom a hand in the venue kitchen with early meal preparation. No one had bothered to put back the tables and chairs after the wedding, saving time in setting those up, although they were being rearranged to accommodate the smaller group. I made sure all the lights were lit, the few leftover centerpieces I'd found on the bar strategically placed, and then I hurried inside to ascertain everything in the house remained in tiptop Christmas-y display. I found Malory and her parents seated in the living room, looking uncomfortable.

"Isn't there something we can do?" Mrs. Hudson

asked.

"Sure," I said. "How are you with a peeler? Mom and Nester could use a hand with the veggies. They're out in the barn kitchen."

Mr. Hudson stood up from his chair as if prodded. "And me? What can I do?"

I felt awful. They'd been left in the kitchen to enjoy breakfast and then, in all the fuss, forgotten. Naturally they wanted to be part of everything. They were family.

"Dad, Shep and Simon are out in the barn, too. They're just shoving tables and chairs around, but I think Dad has a couple things left on his list he could use help with."

Grinning, the Hudsons headed out the door, donning their coats. I could have told them the coats weren't necessary, but I let them go. The trip from front door to barn was a short one and Mom had made sure to turn on the heat to warm up the cavernous room inside. I half-expected Malory to accompany them, but she remained at my side.

I smiled at her. "If I forgot to say so in all the commotion yesterday, congratulations."

"You didn't forget but thank you again." Her hand dropped to her abdomen, settled there. She brushed her

hair away from her face with the other. "This is a very nice thing you're all doing today. Not just for Shep and me, but for everyone."

"We try," I responded with a short laugh.

"I'm serious. I know how hard it sometimes is on Shepherd, not being around his family and old friends. I know how hard it would be for me, were the situation reversed. It's difficult enough I'm not seeing my brother this year. He couldn't come, you see. Has Shep spoken with you yet?"

"About what?"

"Typical." She smiled, her dark blue eyes reflecting the light in the dim room. "My brother is standing in as godfather, and we wanted to know if you would be godmother to our baby. Say you will. I know you'd have to travel to our side of the ocean for the event, but then it would be my turn to welcome you to the home I've always known."

Goodness it was a day for handing out hugs left and right. Malory seemed startled at first by my effusive reaction but quickly returned it, the early but generous baby bump pressing against me. I released her and stepped back. "Feel like helping with the lights? I want to make sure they're all on before people start arriving." I glanced at the mantel clock. "Which should start any minute now. Crap."

Malory laughed, turned away, started with the big evergreen by the window. Bending, she plugged the lights in. "I'm thinking every room has something?" she said, glancing up at me.

"Every single one," I said. "Bathrooms are no exception."

"Lovely. I adore Christmas."

I grinned. "Me, too."

"Could we…could we attend a midnight service here? Do you?"

"I haven't in a good many years," I admitted. "But yeah, let's do that if we can."

I had exaggerated the time, but family did start showing up during the next hour. I spotted two cars pulling in while I was primping the beds and plugging in the window lights in the bedrooms. The early comers, those who lived closest, those bearing food, stood in the parking area clutching containers, undecided whether they should go to the house or straight to the barn. I hurried down the stairs, grabbing Malory's hand in passing and dragging her outside with me.

So began a wondrous day, for Shep and Malory, for my nephews, for all of us. I spent precious time

with people I hadn't seen in ages, people I loved and didn't say so to often enough. Before long, before dinner, talk began about making this gathering a regular, standing occasion at another time during the year. I didn't know if those desires would reach fruition, but I had great fun discussing the possibilities. Once we all slipped away again into our own lives, I figured only a certain few would remember the emotional reaction engendered by our impromptu Christmas Eve gathering. That was okay. We were here now.

In a night filled with laughter and conversation, good food and shared memories, one thing stood out for me more than any other. No matter how infrequently we thought about each other on any given day or during any given year, once together the connection binding us all remained as strong as ever. Family ties, whether blood, marriage or friendship, were exactly that. Family was more than a noun. It also held the connotations of an adjective, with its ability to enrich and enhance simpler terms, and even a verb, if I could have managed to use it as such in a sentence. To family was to be, making the word one of action, of activity, of momentum.

The last turning cogs in my plan clicked into place,

relaxed into place really, as I settled finally and certainly into acceptance. Moving back to the place I'd grown up would be like coming home for the holidays for good. I didn't imagine it would all be wine and roses, or in my case the occasional spritzer and sunflowers gathered warm in the sun, but the connectedness would be there, the feeling I belonged, the deep, underlying welcome we offered everyone for the sake of the season.

I stood by the door, watching them all and drying a few stupid, happy tears from my face. No one showed any indication they wished to leave. Some lived close enough the drive wouldn't be taxing, no matter when they headed out, and the rest who had come had booked a place to stay overnight nearby before making the drive to their homes to celebrate Christmas Day. My gaze followed Mom and Dad on the dance floor, moving to music other than Christmas someone had put on. Simon and Lucy were there, too, as was Stuart, with a cousin's daughter about his age, both making silly faces as they swept dramatically around without cognizance as to the music's slow, steady beat. Shepherd and Malory sat with her parents, Nester nearby lifting her phone to snap photos.

I stood aside in observation because this was how I

conducted my life. I would continue to do so even upon my return to Connor Falls, but never had it meant I wanted to be apart from living. This was just my place, my comfortable place. I remained happy with it, embracing all I saw in my heart and soul nevertheless. I felt that more here, though, than any other place I'd ever lived. I had no need to be in the middle of everything, only within contact distance.

I saw Malory glance at her watch. She turned her head. Looking for me, I realized when she made eye contact and got up from her chair. I met her halfway.

"Church?" she said, when I drew near. "Do you still want to?"

"Sure. Is anyone else interested? Should we ask?"

"Mum and Dad are a bit knackered. And Shep's okay sticking around here. I'm afraid if we start asking we'll break up the party and people will feel uncomfortable with whatever answer they give."

"That makes sense," I agreed. "I'll just let Mom know. It's not a long service, if I remember correctly, so they probably won't even miss us."

Nester ended up accompanying us as well. We three climbed into my little compact and headed out into a night where the stars had begun to disappear behind gauzy clouds. I eyed the sky with a frown as I

turned left from the driveway, heading toward town. "I hope the snow holds off until everyone has made it home. I thought it wasn't supposed to start until midday, but the clouds are already gathering."

"You might end up with more people than you expected for Christmas dinner," Nester stated, quite happily.

"If that happens," said Malory, "we'll all help. It'll be fine."

"I wish we had more time."

Malory and I both glanced at Nester in the back seat. "More time for what?" I asked.

"To stay. I like it here. Also, I would have made a Christmas pudding. I know how, you know. Mum taught me a while ago. How about next year?"

I grinned. "Next year sounds wonderful."

We drove along Main Street at less than the twenty mile per hour limit, because Nester wanted to exclaim over everything she saw. It didn't matter. Traffic was pretty much non-existent. Lights twinkled in windows and on the wreaths hanging from lampposts, bringing another smile to my lips. We parked down the block from the church in the middle of town, as the small parking lot was full, and walked toward the building arm in arm at Nester's insistence. Perhaps her mood

was caused by the season, or her excitement at her first time in the States, but I found her exuberance at sixteen years old utterly delightful. I seemed to recall I had a rather blasé outlook on the world at her age, although time might have managed to warp my perspective in that regard.

The church had been built in 1890 and retained everything of its antiquated charm. Focal lights on the ground illuminated the brick building, painted white before I'd been born, the dual doors with their matching wreaths, the tall steeple with the bell that would shortly be ringing. The light from inside the tall, narrow windows made jewels of the stained glass. At the door, we were given battery-powered tealights to hold. It was a candlelight celebration, modernized for safety's sake. The tiny devices didn't throw much light, but real candles secured in sconces lined the walls, flames flickering, together with electrical fixtures dimmed to accommodate the atmosphere.

Due to Nester's gawking, we'd arrived a bit late and could only find a seat in a back pew. I smelled evergreen and perfume, wood and the paper in the hymnals we took into our hands. Fresh, cold air had wafted in with our entry, clung to our coats, drifted around us to mingle with the other scents.

"So," whispered Nester, leaning close, "is this, like, your church?"

"It was once. A long time ago. I don't live in Connor Falls right now. But I'm moving back."

She nodded. "Good."

The service was almost exactly what I remembered, joyful and triumphant, as the song goes, but also serene, lying gently in the soul. At its conclusion everyone turned, neighbor to neighbor, with wishes for peace and a merry Christmas. Possessing such close proximity to the doors, Malory, Nester and I were some of the first to exit. I stood a moment on the walkway, contented, studying the night sky, the gathering clouds, the stars glimmering beyond dimmed by the town's lights. The church bells rang out above our heads.

"Who's that?" said Nester. I dropped my head, looking at her. "There's a man watching you. Do you know him?"

I followed her gaze, my own lighting without surprise on Arlo. Jenny stood beside him, speaking to another woman. I drew a deep breath. He spotted me as if he'd heard it.

"Here he comes," Nester whispered.

And so he was, once again looking completely at

ease in his suit. I wondered again what he'd done for a living in his prior life. "Susan," he said.

"Arlo," I answered. "This is my sister-in-law, Malory. And this—"

"I'm Nester," said Nester, stepping forward and shaking his hand. "Malory's sister. The younger and better-looking sister."

Her tone said joking, her coy look said flirting. I frowned, only half in amusement. Yet I'd seen that sort of behavior before from young girls when confronted with a charismatic man. Because in his way he was that, even if I hadn't truly noticed it before this moment. She could have been a thirty-something throwing herself at him, rather than a bantering teenager, and I don't think it would have mattered. He seemed to only have eyes for me.

For *me*. He had to stop. He couldn't do that.

"Nice to meet you both," he said, giving Nester and Malory his brief attention and a nod. He glanced toward the church behind us, focusing as I now understood on a level line, and then back down again, straight at me. Jenny hurried up to his side.

"Are you okay? You know how the dark and the street lights—"

"I'm fine," he said, turning to her with a patient

smile. "I told you how much better I am. You've just got to learn to believe me when I say that."

"Hi," said Nester. "Happy Christmas."

Jenny's eyebrows arched. "Hi. Merry Christmas to you, too."

"This is…Nester, right?" Arlo said. "And Malory, and Susan you've met. This is my sister Jenny."

"Your sister," I said, not very loudly. He heard me anyway. So did Nester, who gave me a slow, amused look.

"Sorry, didn't I say?"

I shook my head. "Nope." My lips turned up, almost as if they were a separate entity. I didn't seem able to stop them from doing so. Arlo's expression matched mine in short order, two people smiling at each other for no good reason.

Except maybe there was one. A reason. A darned good reason.

*   *   *

Family headed out early on Christmas Day, not coming by for breakfast, intent on avoiding the snow. It had been more than ten years since Connor Falls had seen a heavy snowfall on Christmas Day and it looked

not to be holding off for the afternoon as had been the original prediction. Some hearty souls with all-wheel drive and not far to travel decided to stick around through the early dinner. We had a contingency plan in case they needed to spend the night. Three (Alice and Herb, who'd brought Gran) would bunk down at Simon and Lucy's, while the rest would take my bed, the bed Nester had slept in, and the sofa in the den. Nester and I agreed to sleeping bags on the back porch. She clearly rooted for the large sleepover.

Another vehicle possessed the equipment to plow through winter weather: Arlo's Jeep. He and Jenny showed up about an hour before mealtime, Jenny at the wheel. I could well imagine how the swirling flakes in his vision might be a problem for Arlo. He'd phoned earlier asking Mom if it would be okay to bring his sister. Seeing the container in Jenny's hand as she climbed out, I understood she came prepared not to be a burden to feed. Not that she would have been. We had more food than needed. I stood out on the porch hugging myself in the cold, watching the two of them interact in the driveway. I don't know how I hadn't recognized the brother-sister thing immediately. Not only in a physical appearance that had, with knowledge, become obvious, but in the way they treated each other.

"Welcome!" I shouted from beneath the sheltering porch roof. Jenny waved with one hand, clutching the Rubbermaid with the other, and still managed to extend her arm toward Arlo. He rolled his eyes at her and ignored the offer, making his way across the snow-covered driveway unaided. They mounted the steps and stopped at the top, stamping snow from their boots. I jerked my head toward the front door, which I'd left cracked a little. Wonderful scents drifted out into the cold air, along with the strains of barely heard music and enough conversation I couldn't determine the content of any.

"Go on in. Nobody bites." I held the screen door open. Jenny pushed the inside door wide and stepped over the threshold. I moved back to let Arlo enter, too. Mom appeared in front of Jenny, ushering her all the way in with a hearty greeting. Before we could follow, she pushed the door closed on Arlo and me. Deliberately and with a look I couldn't mistake. A second later the door opened again and a coat flew out at me. Not mine. I don't think Mom cared whose it was.

"Well," I said, "that couldn't have been any more obvious. Shoot, did I say that out loud?"

"You did."

I took a moment to shove my arms into a coat made for someone taller and broader and carefully fastened the zipper. My cheeks heated.

"It's okay, though," he said.

I grunted.

"Do we have time for a walk?"

I spun toward him, startled. "I—sure. Anyplace in particular?"

His mouth had widened into a grin, his eyes on mine. Steadily. I stayed still so they would, too. I liked him seeing me, although I think he did more often than I realized.

"You're not nervous, are you?" he asked. "You don't seem the type."

He wasn't being coy. The question appeared quite sincere.

"Not at all," I said.

"Show me this place you're thinking of moving into."

My brows lowered. "How do you know about that? Does everyone know about that?"

"Simon," he said. "He gave me your phone number, too. Didn't you wonder where I'd gotten it?"

I laughed. "Yeah, for a hot minute, and then I forgot to ask." I moved to the porch steps, staring out toward the snowy fields and the flakes falling thicker and faster. "Will you need my arm?"

"I don't think so. If I do, I'll let you know?"

"Works for me."

We stepped down from the porch onto the walkway, feet crunching in the frozen residue left behind by his and Jenny's footprints quickly filling in. Snowflakes brushed my cheeks, caught in my hair, my lashes. We walked side by side, the humps and bumps in the field delineated by the snow.

"I like Connor Falls," he said when we were halfway to our destination. No other words had passed between us. I recognized our silence with a start, yet I didn't view it as some telling lack in communication. Things were said that needed to be said. I'd noticed that with him, and I wasn't usually much for small talk anyway. "I've decided to make it my home."

"I like it, too, more than like it, which is why I'm remaking it my home."

"I'm glad." Yes, not small talk. Saying things that he meant to be said.

We reached the place in the woods where Dad and I had cleared the path. I heard nothing but our footsteps, our breathing, the rustle of my borrowed coat and the snowfall's gentle, whispering hush. Together we

entered the narrow path. He dropped behind when we could no longer walk side by side. When we reached the clearing, I swept my hand out toward the building looming like frosted gingerbread. Arlo drew a sudden breath.

He didn't mention how much work it would be, didn't point out the structure's condition, didn't question my sanity. "It's perfect for you," he said.

"I think so." My shoulders settled, dropped in the oversized coat. My breath frosted in a long, slow release. "I had a bird once. A little finch. I named him Guthrie after Arlo Guthrie. You?"

"Same," he said.

"You had a little bird, too?" I teased.

"No. My parents had me. They were fans."

"Of you, I'm sure."

Grinning, I bumped my elbow against his. He smiled and took my hand. We watched the snow gently outline the fieldstone walls, coat the slate roof. An owl hooted nearby. Seeking its mate. A fox darted out from behind the building, auburn flashing through the white.

It was good to be home.

Mary Hardwick's Spearmint Jelly Recipe

This recipe makes about four ½ pint jars. Mary says if you're planning to give them away as gifts, you may wish to double the recipe.

Ingredients

> 1 ½ cups packed mint leaves (fresh)
> 2 tablespoons lemon juice
> 2 ¼ cups boiling water
> 1 drop green food color (optional)
> 3 ½ cups white granulated sugar
> 3 fluid ounces liquid pectin
>
> Four or five ½ pint canning jars

Directions

Rinse off the fresh mint leaves. Place the leaves into a large saucepan and crush with a potato masher. Add the water and bring the mixture to a boil. Remove from the pan from the heat and cover. Let the mint and water stand for approximately ten minutes. Strain the mixture. Measure out a 1 and 2/3 cup of prepared mint. Clean your saucepan.

Place the 1 and 2/3 cup of mint into the cleaned saucepan. Stir in the lemon juice and food coloring. Mix in all the sugar and place the pan over high heat. Bring the mixture to a boil, stirring constantly. Once the mixture has begun to boil, stir the pectin in. Further boil the mixture for a full minute, continuing to stir constantly. Remove the saucepan from the heat and skim the foam off the top of the water using a large metal spoon. Pour the mixture into hot sterilized jars and seal.

Place a rack in the bottom of a large pot. Fill the pot halfway with water and bring the water to a boil. Carefully lower the canning jars with the jelly into the pot using a potholder, tongs, or some other utensil. Leave approximately two inches between the jars. If necessary, add more boiling water in order to assure the water level is about one inch above the sealed jar lids. Bring the water to a full boil, cover the pot, and let boil for ten minutes.

Take the pot off the heat and set on heat-safe surface. Safely remove the jars from the water, setting them on a flat heat-safe surface to cool. Leave them sealed until use. Do not make if you are allergic.

Shelly's *Back to the Garden* Salad

Ingredients

> Greens (fresh leaf lettuce, fresh romaine, fresh spinach, etc. washed and prepared), enough to fill a large serving bowl
> 1 cup fresh, washed and sliced strawberries
> 1 cup fresh, washed blueberries
> 1 cup dried cranberries
> ¾ cup peeled mandarin segments
> ¾ cup candied pecans
> ¾ to 1 cup crumbled goat cheese
> ½ cup chopped walnuts
> ½ to ¾ cup dressing (your choice)

Directions

Chill all ingredients until ready to serve.

Combine the ingredients (except dressing) in a large serving bowl. Any ingredient is optional, but together they are delicious. Pour your favorite dressing over all and toss when ready to eat. (Strawberry vinaigrette is great with this salad.) Of course, if you are allergic to any ingredient, definitely leave it out. Enjoy!

Titles in the Connor Falls Christmas Series:

Hurry Home for Christmas
Connor Falls Christmas Book One

I Knew in a Moment
Connor Falls Christmas Book Two

Winter Light
A Connor Falls Christmas Novella

Light the Heart Home
A Connor Falls Christmas Novella

Home for the Holidays
A Connor Falls Christmas Novella

When the Heart Brings You Home
A Connor Falls Christmas Collection containing
Winter Light, *Light the Heart Home* and *Home for the Holidays* in one volume